"I can tell wher
Your eyes grow
corner of your mouth tightens."

Would his mouth be hard or soft, passionate or gentle against hers when they kissed?

"I don't want you," he said as he moved closer to her lips.

"You're bluffing."

"You're too trusting." He lowered his mouth to her ear. "But I don't have the strength to pull away."

She smiled. "Now you're telling the truth."

With a groan he fastened his lips to hers. She didn't hesitate. She clung to him and let his mouth drive away the memories of the past week. For this wonderful moment all she could think about was his touch.

He lifted his head. "Be very sure, because I won't let you go all night long."

CHRISTMAS JUSTICE

ROBIN PERINI

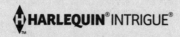

With love to my aunts, Gayle, Earlene, Sissy (Lynn)
and Barbara. I'm blessed to know you are always there.
No matter what.

Recycling programs
for this product may
not exist in your area.

ISBN-13: 978-0-373-69803-5

Christmas Justice

Copyright © 2014 by Robin L. Perini

All rights reserved. Except for use in any review, the reproduction or
utilization of this work in whole or in part in any form by any electronic,
mechanical or other means, now known or hereinafter invented, including
xerography, photocopying and recording, or in any information storage
or retrieval system, is forbidden without the written permission of the
publisher, Harlequin Enterprises Limited, 225 Duncan Mill Road,
Don Mills, Ontario M3B 3K9, Canada.

This is a work of fiction. Names, characters, places and incidents are
either the product of the author's imagination or are used fictitiously,
and any resemblance to actual persons, living or dead, business
establishments, events or locales is entirely coincidental.

This edition published by arrangement with Harlequin Books S.A.

For questions and comments about the quality of this book,
please contact us at CustomerService@Harlequin.com.

® and ™ are trademarks of Harlequin Enterprises Limited or its
corporate affiliates. Trademarks indicated with ® are registered in the
United States Patent and Trademark Office, the Canadian Intellectual
Property Office and in other countries.

Printed in U.S.A.

www.Harlequin.com

ABOUT THE AUTHOR

Award-winning author Robin Perini's love of heart-stopping suspense and poignant romance, coupled with her adoration of high-tech weaponry and covert ops, encouraged her secret inner commando to take on the challenge of writing romantic suspense novels. Her mission's motto: "When danger and romance collide, no heart is safe."

Devoted to giving her readers fast-paced, high-stakes adventures with a love story sure to melt their hearts, Robin won a prestigious Romance Writers of America Golden Heart Award in 2011. By day she works for an advanced technology corporation, and in her spare time you might find her giving one of her many nationally acclaimed writing workshops or training in competitive small-bore-rifle silhouette shooting. Robin loves to interact with readers. You can catch her on her website, www.robinperini.com, and on several major social-networking sites, or write to her at PO Box 50472, Albuquerque, NM 87181-0472.

Books by Robin Perini

Other titles by this author available in ebook format.
Don't miss any of our special offers. Write to us at the following address for information on our newest releases.

Harlequin Reader Service
U.S.: 3010 Walden Ave., P.O. Box 1325, Buffalo, NY 14269
Canadian: P.O. Box 609, Fort Erie, Ont. L2A 5X3

CAST OF CHARACTERS

Laurel McCallister—She witnessed her sister's family murdered. Can the man whose name her sister whispered with her last breath protect Laurel—and her five-year-old niece—from the determined men who want them dead?

Sheriff Garrett Galloway—He lost his family in an explosion that nearly took his life. Now the past has returned. Can he protect Laurel and Molly—or will those out to destroy him finally get what they want?

James McCallister—Missing for two months, he is the only person who knows Garrett's true identity. Has he been forced to betray not only Garrett, but his daughters, as well?

Deputy Keller—Will his inexperience and doubts cost Garrett and Laurel their lives?

Fiona Wylde—Garrett and Laurel don't want to place anyone else in danger, but could Fiona hold the key to James McCallister's whereabouts and the identity of the traitor?

Mike Strickland—He'll eliminate anyone who gets in his way, but even he doesn't want to face the traitor who calls the shots.

Derek Bradley—This traitor is supposed to be dead. What will happen when the truth is exposed?

Hondo Rappaport—A man with his own mysteries, he helped Garrett and Laurel escape Trouble, Texas. Will Hondo betray them to save his sister?

Covert Technology Confidential (CTC)—This organization of elite warriors helps those who have run out of options. But has the team met its match?

Prologue

Today was no ordinary day.

Normally Laurel McCallister would have adored spending an evening with her niece Molly, playing princesses, throwing jacks and just being a kid again, but tonight was anything but typical. Laurel let the wind-driven ice bite into her cheeks. She stood just inside the warm entry of her sister's Virginia home, staring out into the weather to see the family off to the local Christmas pageant. Her fist clutched the charm bracelet Ivy had forced into Laurel's hand.

A gift from their missing father.

He'd been incommunicado for over two months. Then suddenly the silver jewelry had arrived in Ivy's mailbox earlier that day. No note, only her father's shaky handwriting on the address label, and postmarked Washington, D.C. Laurel squeezed the chain, quelling the shiver of foreboding that hadn't left her since Ivy had shown her the package. Her sister had told her they needed to talk about it. Tonight. The news couldn't be good, but it would have to wait.

Bracing against the cold, she met her sister's solemn gaze, then picked up her five-year-old niece. Laurel snuggled Molly closer. At the end of a bout of strep throat, the girl had insisted on waving goodbye to her mother. Ivy returned the farewell wave from across the driveway, apprehension evident in her eyes. And not typical mom-concern-for-her-youngest-daughter's-health worry.

Laurel scanned the rural setting surrounding Ivy's house. With the nearest neighbors out of shouting distance, it should be quiet. And safe. Laurel might only be a CIA analyst, but she'd completed the same training as a field operative. She knew what to look for.

Nothing seemed off, and yet, she couldn't stop the tension knotting every muscle, settling low in her belly. For now, her sister and brother-in-law refused to let the trepidation destroy Christmas for the kids, but Laurel had recognized the strain in her sister's eyes, the worry on her brother-in-law's brow. Too many bad vibes filtered beneath the surface of every look her sister had given her.

Laurel touched the silky blond hair of her youngest niece.

Molly stared after her mother, father, brother and sister, her baby blues filled with tears. "It's not fair. I want to go to the pageant. I'm supposed to be an angel."

The forlorn voice hung on Laurel's heart. She placed her hand on the little girl's hot forehead. "Sorry, Molly Magoo. Not with that fever."

Ivy bundled Molly's older brother and sister into the backseat of the car. Laurel sent her sister a confident nod, even though her stomach still twisted. She recognized the same lie in her sister's eyes. They were so alike.

One of the kids—it must have been Michaela—tossed a stuffed giraffe through the open car door. Ivy shook her head and walked a few paces away to pick up the wayward animal.

Laurel started to close the door. "Don't worry, Molly. They'll be back s—"

A loud explosion rocketed the night, and a blast of hot air buffeted Laurel. She staggered back. The driver's side of the SUV erupted into flames. Fire and smoke engulfed the car in a hellish conflagration. Angry black plumes erupted into the sky.

God, no! Laurel's knees trembled; she shook her head. This couldn't be happening. Horror squeezed her throat. She wrenched Molly toward her, turning the little girl away from the sight, but Laurel couldn't protect Molly. Her niece had seen too much. Molly's earsplitting screams ripped the air.

No sounds came from the car. Not a shout, not a yell.

Laurel had to do *something*.

"Stay here!" She scrambled through the door, racing across the frozen yard. She glanced back; Molly had fallen to the floor in tears. Laurel squeezed her eyes shut against the heart-wrenching cries, then snagged her phone from her pocket and dialed 9-1-1. "Help! There's been an explosion."

Blazing heat seared Laurel's skin. It wasn't a typical car fire. It burned too hot, too fast. Laurel choked back the truth. This wasn't just any bomb. This was a professional hit. A hit like she'd read about in dossiers as part of her job with the CIA.

Unable to look away, she stared in horror at the interior of the car. In a few minutes, nothing would be left. Just ash. They wouldn't even be able to tell how many people had been in the car.

The phone slipped from her fingers.

Ivy's family was gone. No one could have survived. Frantically, Laurel searched for her sister. Her heart shattered when she saw the smoking body lying several feet away from the car. She ran to Ivy and knelt next to her sister's body, the right side blackened and burned beyond recognition, the left blistered and smoldering.

"Laur—" the raspy voice croaked.

"Don't talk, Ivy." Laurel couldn't stop her tears. She could hear her niece's wails from inside the house, but Ivy. God. Her clothes had melted into her skin.

Ivy shifted, then cried out in agony. "Stupid," she rasped. "Not c-c-careful enough. Can't...trust..."

"Shh..." Laurel had no idea how to help. She reached out a hand, but there wasn't a spot on Ivy not burned. She was afraid to touch her sister. Where was the ambulance?

Ivy coughed and Laurel bent down. "Don't give up. Help is coming."

"Too late. F-find Garrett Galloway. Sheriff. Tell him... he was right." Ivy blinked her one good eye and glanced at the fire-consumed vehicle. A lone tear pooled. "Please. Save. Molly." The single tear cut through the soot, and then her eyes widened. "Gun!"

Laurel's training took over. She plastered herself flat to the ground. A shot hit the tree behind her. With a quick roll, she cursed. Her weapon was locked up in the gun safe inside the house. A loud thwack hit the ground inches from her ear. The assault had come from the hedges.

"Traitor!" Ivy's raspy voice shouted a weak curse.

Another shot rang out.

The bullet struck true, hitting Ivy right in the temple.

Horrified, Laurel scampered a few feet, using the fire as a shield between her and the gunman. She panted, ignoring the pain ripping through her heart. She would grieve later. She had one job: protect Molly.

Sirens roared through the night sky. A curse rang out followed by at least two sets of footsteps, the sound diminishing.

Thank God they'd run. Laurel had one chance. She flung open the door and grabbed a sobbing Molly in her arms. She hugged her tight, then kicked the door closed.

Through the break in the curtains, she watched. A squad car tore into the driveway. No way. That cop had gotten here way too fast. Laurel pressed Molly against her, then locked the dead bolt.

She sagged against the wall. "Oh, Ivy."

"Aunt Laurel?" Molly's small voice choked through her sobs. "I want Mommy and Daddy."

"Me, too, pumpkin."

Laurel squeezed her niece tighter. She had two choices: trust the cop outside or follow her sister's advice.

After the past two months… She slipped the bracelet from her father into her pocket, then snagged a photo from the wall. Her sister and family, all smiles. She had no choice. The high-tech bomb, the cop's quick arrival. It smelled of setup.

Laurel raced through the house and grabbed Molly's antibiotics and the weapon from the gun safe, half expecting the cop to bang on the door. When he didn't, Laurel knew she was right. She peeked through the curtains. Her sister's body was gone. And so was the police car.

The flames sparked higher and Laurel nearly doubled over in pain.

The sound of a fire engine penetrated the house. No time left. She snagged the envelope her father had sent and stuffed it into a canvas bag along with a blanket and Molly's favorite stuffed lion.

She bundled Molly into her coat, lifted her niece into her arms and ran out the back door. Laurel's feet slapped on the pavement. She sprinted down an alley. Shouts rained down on her. Smoke and fire painted the night sky in a vision of horror. One she would never forget.

She paused, catching her breath, the cold seeping through her jacket.

"Aunt Laurel? Stop. Mommy won't know where to find us." Molly's fingers dug into Laurel's neck.

Oh, God. Poor Molly. Laurel hugged her niece closer. How could she explain to a five-year-old about bad people who killed families?

Laurel leaned against the concrete wall, her lungs burning with effort. She wished *she* didn't understand. She wished she could be like Molly. But this wasn't a child's cartoon where everyone survived even the most horrendous attacks. Reality meant no one had a second chance.

Laurel had to get away from the men who had shot at her, who had killed her sister and her family.

But Laurel didn't know what to believe. Except her sister's final words.

Which left her with one option. One man to trust.

Garrett Galloway.

Now all she had to do was find him.

Chapter One

Normally Trouble, Texas, wasn't much trouble, and that was the way Sheriff Garrett Galloway liked it. No problems to speak of, save the town drunk, a few rambunctious kids and a mayor who drove too nice a car with no obvious supplemental income.

Garrett adjusted his Stetson and shoved his hands into the pockets of his bomber jacket to ward off the December chill. He'd hidden out in Trouble too long. When he'd arrived a year ago, body broken and soul bleeding, he'd trusted that the tiny West Texas town would be the perfect place to get lost and stay lost for a few months. After all, the world thought he was dead. And Garrett needed it to stay that way.

Just until he could identify who had destroyed everyone he loved and make them pay. He'd *never* imagined he'd stay this long.

But the latest status call he'd counted on hadn't occurred. Not to mention his last conversation with his mentor and ex-partner, James McCallister, had been much too...optimistic. That, combined with a missed contact, usually meant the operation had gone to hell.

Garrett's right shoulder blade hiked, settling under the feel of his holster. He never left home without his weapon or his badge. He liked to know he had a gun within reach. Always. The townsfolk liked to know their sheriff walked the streets.

He eyed the garland- and tinsel-laden but otherwise empty Main Street and stepped onto the pavement, his boots silent, no sound echoing, no warning to anyone that he might be making his nightly nine o'clock rounds.

James McCallister's disappearance had thrown Garrett. His mentor had spent the past few months using every connection he'd made over his nearly thirty-year career, trying to ferret out the traitor.

Big risks, but after a year of nothing, a few intel tidbits had fallen their way: some compromised top secret documents identifying overseas operatives and operations, some missing state-of-the-art weapons. The door had cracked open, but not enough to step through.

Garrett didn't like the radio silence. Either James was breaking open the case or he was dead. Neither option boded well. If it was the first, Garrett contacting him would blow the whole mission; if the second, Garrett was on his own and would have to come back from the dead.

Or he could end up in federal prison, where his life wouldn't be worth a spare .22 bullet.

With his no-win options circling his mind, Garrett strode past another block. After a few more houses, he spied an unfamiliar dark car slowly making its way down the street.

No one drove that slowly. Not in Texas. Not unless they were up to no good. And no one visited Trouble without good reason. It wasn't a town folks passed through by chance.

His instincts firing warning signals, Garrett turned the corner and disappeared behind a hedge.

The car slowed, then drove past. Interesting.

Could be a relative from out of town, but Garrett didn't like changes. Or the unexpected. He headed across a dead-end street, his entire body poised and tense, watching for the car. He reached the edge of town and peered through the deserted night.

Nearby, he heard a small crack, as if a piece of wood snapped.

No one should be out this way, not at this time of night. Could be a coyote—human, not the animal variety. Garrett hadn't made friends with either one during the past year.

He slid his Beretta 92 from his shoulder holster and gripped the butt of the gun. Making a show of a cowboy searching the stars, he gazed up at the black expanse of the night sky and pushed his Stetson back.

Out of the corner of his eye, he caught sight of a cloaked figure ducking behind a fence: average height, slight, but the movements careful, strategic, trained. Someone he might have faced in his previous life. Definitely. Not your average coyote or even criminal up to no good. James Mc-Callister was the only person who knew Garrett was in Trouble, and James was AWOL.

The night went still.

Garrett kicked the dirt and dusted off his hat.

His muscles twitchy, he kept his gun at the ready, not wanting to use it. This could be unrelated to his past, but he needed information, not a dead body on the outskirts of his town. What happened in Trouble stayed in Trouble, unless the body count started climbing. Then he wouldn't be able to keep the state or the feds out.

He didn't need the attention.

He could feel someone watching him, studying him.

He veered off his route, heading slightly toward the hidden figure. His plan? Saunter past the guy hiding in the shadows and then take him out.

He hit his mark and, with a quick turn on his heel, shifted, launching himself into a tackle. A few quick moves and Garrett pushed the guy to the ground, slid the SIG P229 out of reach and forced his forearm against the vulnerable section of throat.

"What do you want?" he growled, shoving aside his pinned assailant's hood.

The grunts coming from his victim weren't what he'd expected. With years of experience subduing the worst human element, he wrestled free his flashlight and clicked it on.

Blue eyes full of fear peered up at him. A woman. He pressed harder. A woman could kill just as dead. Could play the victim, all the while coldheartedly planning his demise. He wasn't about to let go.

The light hit her face. He blinked back his surprise. He knew those eyes. Knew that nose.

Oh, hell.

"Laurel McCallister," he said. His gut sank. Only one thing would bring her to Trouble.

His past had found him. And that meant one thing. James McCallister was six feet under, and the men who wanted Garrett dead wouldn't be far behind.

THE PAVEMENT DUG into Laurel's back, but she didn't move, not with two hundred pounds holding her down. He'd taken her SIG too easily, and the man lying on top of her knew how to kill. The pressure against her throat proved it.

Worse than that, the sheriff—badge and all—knew her name. So much for using surprise as an advantage.

She lay still and silent, her body jarred from his attack. She could feel every inch of skin and muscle that had struck the ground. She'd be bruised later.

Laurel had thought watching him for a while would be a good idea. Maybe not so much. Ivy might have told her to trust Garrett Galloway, Sheriff of Trouble, Texas, but Laurel had to be cautious.

The car door opened and the thud of tiny feet pounded to them. "Let her go!" Molly pummeled Garrett's back, her raised voice screeching through the night in that high-pitched kid squeal that raked across Laurel's nerves.

He winced and turned to the girl.

Now!

Laurel kicked out, her foot coming in contact with his shin. He grunted, but didn't budge. She squirmed underneath the heavy body and pushed at his shoulders.

"Molly, get back!"

The little girl hesitated, sending a shiver of fear through Laurel. Why couldn't her niece have stayed asleep in the car, buckled into her car seat? Ever since that horrific night four days ago, she couldn't handle Laurel being out of sight, knew instinctively when she wasn't near.

Suddenly, Garrett rolled off her body, slipped her gun into his hand and rose to his feet with cougarlike grace. "Don't worry. I'm not going to hurt either of you." He tucked her weapon into his pants and stared her down.

She sucked in a wary breath before her five-year-old niece dived into her arms. "Are you okay, Aunt Laurel?"

She wound her arms around her niece and stared up at Garrett, body tense. "You're my hero, Molly." She forced her voice to remain calm. At least the little girl hadn't lost the fire in her belly. It was the first spark Laurel had seen from her since the explosion.

Molly clutched at Laurel but glared at Garrett.

He struggled to keep a straight face and a kindness laced his eyes as he looked at Molly.

For the first time in days, the muscles at the base of Laurel's neck relaxed. Maybe she'd made the right decision after all.

Not that she'd had a choice. There'd been nothing on the national news about her family. No mention of gunfire or Ivy being killed by a bullet to the head. There had been a small piece about an SUV burning, but they'd blamed a downed power line. That was the second Laurel had known she was truly on her own.

Until now.

She hated counting on anyone but herself. She and her sister had been schooled in that lesson after their mother had died. With their father gone, Ivy and Laurel had been pretty much in charge of each other.

But Laurel was out of her league. She knew it. She didn't have to like it.

She held Molly closer and studied Garrett Galloway. Something about him invited trust, but could she trust her instincts? Would this man whose expression displayed an intent to kill one moment and compassion the next help her? She prayed her sister had been right, that he was one of the good guys.

Garrett tilted back his Stetson. "I could have…" He glanced at Molly, his meaning clear.

Laurel got it. She and Molly would be dead…if he'd wanted them dead.

"…already finished the job," he said harshly. "I'm not going to."

"How did you know my name?"

He raised a brow and slipped his Beretta into the shoulder holster and returned her weapon. "I know your father. Your picture is on his desk at…work."

His expression spoke volumes. She got it. Garrett had worked with her father in an OGA. While the CIA had a name and a reputation, her father's Other Government Agency had none. Classified funding, classified missions, classified results. And the same agency where Ivy had worked. Alarm bells rang in Laurel's head. Her sister had sent Laurel to a man working with the same people who might be behind the bomb blast. And yet, who better to help?

Garrett held out his hand to her. "You look like you've been on the road awhile," he said. "How about something to eat? Then we can talk."

Laurel hesitated, but what was she supposed to do? She'd come to this small West Texas town for one reason, and one reason only. To find Garrett Galloway.

She didn't know what she'd expected. He could have stepped off the set of a hit television show in his khaki shirt, badge, dark brown hat and leather jacket. Piercing brown eyes that saw right through her.

If she'd imagined wanting to ride off into the sunset with someone, it would be Garrett Galloway. But now that she'd found him, what *was* she going to do with him?

He didn't pull back his hand. He waited. He knew. With a sigh, she placed her hand in his. He pulled her to her feet. Molly scrambled up and hid behind Laurel, peering up at Garrett.

He cocked his head at the little girl. Laurel sucked in

a slow breath. Molly's face held that fearful expression that hadn't left her since they'd run from Virginia, as if any second she might cry. But then her eyes widened. She stared at Garrett, so tall and strong in his dark pants and cowboy boots, a star on his chest.

He was a protector. Laurel could tell and so, evidently, could Molly.

Garrett met her gaze and she recognized the understanding on his face. "Come with me," he said quietly.

"I have my car—"

He shook his head. "Grab your things and leave it. If anyone followed, I don't want them to know who you came to see."

"I was careful. I spent an entire extra day to get here due to all the detours."

"If you'd recognized you had a tail, you'd already be dead." His flat words spoke the truth of the danger they were in. He walked over to the vehicle and pulled out the large tote she used as a suitcase, slinging it on his shoulder opposite his gun hand. All their belongings were in the bag. "Until I'm certain, we act like you have one."

Laurel stiffened. In normal circumstances she could take care of herself and Molly. As if sensing her vulnerability, Garrett stepped closer.

"*You* came to *me*," Garrett said. "You may have blown my cover. You need to listen."

He was on assignment. She should have known.

She prided herself on her self-reliance, her ability to handle most any situation, but his expression had gone intense and wary, and that worried her. Ivy had been a skilled operative. She had always been careful, and she was dead. Laurel had to face reality. She'd jumped into the deep end of the pool her first day on the run and Garrett Galloway was the lifeguard.

She swallowed away the distaste of having to rely on him, nodded and lifted Molly into her arms. "How far?"

"Across town," he said, his gaze scanning the perimeter yet again.

"A few blocks, then?" Laurel said with an arch of her brow.

Garrett cocked his head and one side of his mouth tilted in a small smile. His eyes lightened when he didn't frown.

"Let's go."

One block under their feet had Laurel's entire body pulsing with nerves. She'd never seen anyone with the deadly focus that Garrett possessed. He walked silently, even in boots, and seemed aware of each shadow and movement.

Suddenly he stopped. He shoved her and Molly back against the fence, pulling his gun out. Then she heard it. The purr of an engine. It grew louder, then softer. He relaxed and tilted his head, looking from Laurel to Molly. "Let's move."

Molly gazed up at him, her eyes wide. She looked ready to cry. He tilted the Stetson on his head. "You ready for something to eat, sugar?" He gifted her with a confident smile.

Just his strong presence soothed Molly. For Laurel, his nearness had the opposite effect. She wanted to pull away, because the draw she felt—the odd urge to let herself move into his arms—well, that was something she hadn't felt before. She'd never allowed herself to be this vulnerable. Not ever.

He could snap her neck or take her life, but he might

also do worse. This man could take over and she might lose herself.

A dog's howl broke through the night, followed by more barking. As Garrett led them through the town in silence, Molly clung to Laurel. Her eyes grew heavy and her body lax. The poor thing was exhausted, just like her aunt.

Garrett matched his steps with hers. "Whatever brought you here, it was bad, wasn't it?" He bent toward Laurel, his breath near her ear, the words soft.

She couldn't stop the burning well of tears behind her eyes. She had no reserves left. She wanted nothing more than to lean closer and have him put his arm around her. She couldn't. She recognized her weakness. Her emotions hovered just beneath the surface, and she'd be damned if she'd let them show.

In self-preservation, she tilted her head forward, expecting her long hair to curtain her face, to hide her feelings, but nothing happened. She ran a hand through the chopped locks. Gone was her unique titian hair, and in its place, she'd dyed it a nondescript brown that stopped at her chin. She had to blend in.

"I understand," he said, his voice gruff. "Better than you know."

Before Laurel could ponder his statement, he picked up the pace. "My house is ten minutes away. Across Main and around a corner two blocks."

With each step they took, the blinking lights and garlands, then the tinsel, came into full effect. He paused and shifted them behind a tree, studying the street.

Molly peered around him, her small mouth forming a stunned O. "Aunt Laurel, lookie. It's Christmas here." The little girl swallowed and bowed her head until it rested on Laurel's shoulder. "Our Christmas is far away."

Laurel patted her niece's back. "Christmas will follow us, Molly Magoo. It might be different this year, but it will still happen."

Molly looked at her, then at the decorations lining the town, her gaze hopeful. "Will Mommy and Daddy come back by then?"

"We'll talk about it later," Laurel whispered. She didn't know what to say. Even though Molly had seen the explosion, she still hadn't processed the reality that her mother, father, brother and sister were never coming back.

She gritted her teeth. As a grown woman, she didn't know how long it would take her to accept her family's death. That she was alone in the world. Except for Molly.

"We need to move fast." Garrett held out his arm. Main Street through Trouble wasn't much. Two lanes, a single stoplight. "Go." They were halfway to the other side when an engine roared to life. Tires squealed; the vehicle thundered directly at them.

Garrett pushed them behind a cinder-block wall, dumped the tote, then rolled to the ground, leaving himself vulnerable.

A spray of gunfire ratcheted above Laurel's head as she hit the ground. Molly cried out. Laurel covered the little girl's trembling body and pulled her weapon. She lifted her head, scooting forward. To get a clean shot, she'd have to leave Molly. Bullets thwacked; concrete chips rained down. Laurel tucked Molly closer, gripping the butt of her gun.

A series of shots roared from behind the wall.

Skidding tires took off.

At the sound, Laurel eased forward, weapon raised. She half expected the worst, but Garrett lay on the ground, still alive, his gun aimed at the retreating SUV. He squeezed off two more rounds, then let out a low curse.

She couldn't catch her breath. They'd found her.

"What's going on out there?" An old man's voice called out, and the unmistakable sound of a pump-action shotgun seared through the dark.

"I'm handling it, Mr. McCreary," Garrett called out. "It's Sheriff Galloway. Get back inside."

A door slammed.

Garrett held his weapon at the ready for several more seconds, then picked up his phone. "Shots fired just off Oak and First, Keller," he said to his deputy. "Activate the emergency system and order everyone to stay inside. I'll get back to you when it's clear."

He shoved the phone in his pocket and ran to Laurel. "Everybody safe?"

Molly sobbed in Laurel's arms. She clutched the girl tighter. Laurel didn't know how much more her niece could take.

"Come on." Tension lining his face, he scooped up Molly. His boots thudded on the ground; Laurel carried their belongings and her footsteps pounded closely behind. He led them down an alley to the rear of a row of houses. Then, when he reached the back of one house, he pulled a set of keys from his pocket. "We've got to get out of sight. Plus, I have supplies to gather. Then we need a safe place to hole up."

"I'm sorry," she said quietly. "I brought this to you."

He gave a curt nod. "Who knew you were coming to Texas?"

"No—no one."

"Who told you about me? Your father?" Garrett said.

"My…my sister."

"Ivy?" Garrett's brow furrowed. "She worked for the agency, but we never tackled an op together."

Laurel bit her lip. "My sister said your name with her dying breath. She said to tell you that you were right."

THE SUV THUNDERED down the highway and out of Trouble. Mike Strickland slammed his foot on the accelerator and veered onto an old dirt road leading into the hellish West Texas desert. When he finally brought the vehicle to a halt, he slammed it into Park and pounded the steering wheel with his fist. "Son of a bitch. Who was that guy?"

"The law," his partner, Don Krauss, said, his tone dry. "You see the badge?"

Krauss could pass for everyman. He was great to have on the job because he excelled at blending into the background. His medium brown hair, medium eyes, medium height and nothing-special face got lost in a crowd.

Strickland had a tougher time. A scar from his marine stint and his short hair pegged him as ex-military. He could live with that. He tended to work the less subtle jobs anyway. But Krauss came in handy for gathering intel.

"No sheriff has reflexes like that," Strickland said. "She should be dead. They both should be."

"The girl avoided us for four days, and she's just an analyst, even if she does work for the CIA. She's smart. Switched vehicles twice and never turned on her cell phone." Krauss tapped the high-tech portable triangulation unit.

All this equipment and a girl in a beat-up Chevy had driven over halfway across the country and avoided them. "She got lucky." Strickland frowned.

Krauss let out a snort. "No, we got lucky when she used her ATM for cash. The only stupid move she made, but she cleaned out her account. We won't be lucky again. And now she's got help." He hitched his foot on the dash. "If Ivy talked—"

"I know, I know." Strickland scratched his palm in a nervous movement. In four days the skin had peeled, leaving it red, angry and telling. Not much made him nervous, but his boss... He forced his hand still and gripped the steering wheel, clenching and unclenching his fists against the vinyl. "We can fix this. Forensics will be sifting through what's left of that car for weeks. I made sure it burned hot, and I've got friends in the local coroner's office. If they stall long enough for us to provide two more burned bodies, no one will ever know. Everyone will believe the woman and girl died that night along with the rest of her family."

"You blew her head off," Krauss said. "Cops had to notice."

"It hasn't been on the news, has it?" Strickland said with a small smile.

Krauss shook his head. "I figured they were holding back details as part of the investigation."

"Hell, no. First guy there threw her into the fire. Everyone else is keeping mum. They think it's *national security.*"

"Lots of loose ends, Strickland."

"I got enough on my contacts' extracurricular activities. They won't be talking anytime soon. They know the rules." Strickland slid a glance at his partner. "You read the paper? Remember last year, that dead medical investigator? I had no choice. He was a loose end. Like the boss says, loose ends make for bad business."

Krauss tugged a toothpick from his pocket. "Guess the boss was right in choosing you for this one, because we have two very big loose ends." He turned in the seat, his normally sardonic expression solemn. "You ever wonder how we ended up working for that psycho? 'Cause I'm starting to regret every job we do."

"For the greater good—" Strickland started, his entire back tensing. He cricked his neck to the side.

"Yeah, I might have believed that once," Krauss said.

"Don't." Strickland cut him off. "Don't say something I'll have to report."

"Says the man who's hiding his screwup."

"I don't plan to be on the receiving end of a lesson," Strickland said. "You talk and we're dead. Hell, we're dead if we don't fix this."

"I know," Krauss said, his voice flat. "I got a family to protect. Let's get it done fast, clean up and get the hell out of this town. I already hate Trouble, Texas."

"No witnesses. Agreed?" Strickland turned the motor on.

"The sheriff, too? Could cause some publicity."

"This close to the border, this isolated, there's lots of ways to die."

Chapter Two

"*I was right.* Great, just great," Garrett said under his breath, cradling a sobbing Molly in his arms.

He rocked her slightly. She tucked her head against his shoulder and gripped his neck, her little fingers digging into his hair. He held her tighter while his narrowed gaze scrutinized the alley behind his house. A chill bit through the night, and Molly shivered in his arms. He needed to get them both inside and warm, but not in the place he'd never called home.

Another thirty seconds passed. No movement. The shooter probably didn't have an accomplice, but he couldn't assume anything. Assumptions got people dead.

A quick in and out. That was all he needed.

He led Laurel into the backyard of the house James McCallister had purchased on Garrett's behalf and closed the gate. He wouldn't be returning anytime soon. His time in Trouble had ended the moment he'd tackled Laurel to the ground.

But he needed his go-bag and a few supplies. On his own, it wouldn't have mattered. He shifted Molly's weight in his arms. These two needed more shelter than to camp out in the West Texas desert in December.

Molly clung to him tightly. He rubbed her back and

his heart shifted in his chest. God, so familiar. The memories of his daughter, Ella, flooded back. Along with the pain. He couldn't let the past overcome him. Not with these two needing him. He led them to the wood stack.

"Give me a minute," he whispered. "Stay out of sight, and I'll be right back."

He tried to pass Molly to Laurel, but the little girl whimpered and gripped him even tighter.

"It's okay, sugar. Your aunt Laurel will take good care of you."

With one last pat, he handed Molly to Laurel, his arms feeling strangely empty without the girl's weight. Laurel settled her niece in her arms, her expression pained. He understood. "She's just afraid," he said.

"I know, and I haven't protected her." Laurel hunkered down behind the woodpile. She pulled out her pistol. "I won't fail again."

Laurel McCallister had grit, that was for sure. He liked that about her. "I'll be back soon."

He sped across the backyard, slipped the key into the lock and did a quick sweep of the house, eyeing any telling details. He couldn't leave a trace behind. Nothing to lead any unwelcome visitors to his small cattle ranch in the Guadalupes or to his stashed money and vehicle.

Garrett pressed a familiar number on his phone.

"Sheriff? What happened? Practically the whole town is calling me." Deputy Keller's voice shook a bit.

"Old man McCreary's not putting a posse together, right?" Garrett had a few old-timers in this town who thought they lived in the 1800s. This part of Texas could still be wild, but not *that* wild.

"I talked his poker buddies out of encouraging him,"

Keller said. "It's weird ordering my old high school principal around."

Garrett pocketed a notebook and a receipt or two, then headed straight for his bedroom. "Look, Keller, I'll be incommunicado tracking this guy. I don't want to shoot anyone by mistake. Keep them indoors."

"You need me, Sheriff?"

"Man the phones and keep your eyes out for strangers, Deputy. Don't go after them, Keller. Just call me."

"Yes, sir."

Garrett ended the call. If the men following Laurel and Molly had a mission, his town was safe. Assassins tended to have singular focus. He probably wasn't the target, except as an opportunity. Still, Ivy had known his name. She'd said he was right. He couldn't be certain how much of his identity had been compromised.

If anyone had associated Derek Bradley with Garrett Galloway before today, he'd already be dead. He *might* still have surprise on his side, but he couldn't count on it. And if he'd been right…well, that was all fine. It didn't make him feel any better. There was a traitor in the agency, and he didn't know who. Ivy's message hadn't identified the perp.

Garrett grabbed his go-bag from the closet, then opened a drawer in his thrift-store dresser. He eased out an old, faded photo from beneath the drawer liner.

"It'll be over soon." He glanced at the images he'd stared at for a good two hours after his shift earlier. Hell, it was almost Christmas.

Tomboy that she'd been, his daughter, Ella, would have been after him about a new football or a basketball hoop, while Lisa would've rolled her eyes and wondered when her daughter might want the princess dress—or any dress, for that matter. His throat tightened. He'd never know what kind of woman Ella would have become. Her life had ended before it had begun.

Garrett missed them so much. Every single day. He'd survived the injuries from the explosion for one reason—to make whoever had murdered his family pay. He wouldn't stop until he'd achieved his goal. He'd promised them. He'd promised himself.

He ground his teeth and stuffed the photo into the pocket of his bag. The perps should already be dead. He and James had failed for eighteen months and now… what the hell had happened? Now James's daughter Ivy had paid the ultimate price. And Laurel was on the run.

James was… Who knew where his mentor was?

The squeak of the screen door ricocheted through the house. He'd been inside only a few minutes. He slipped his gun from his shoulder holster and rounded into the hall, weapon ready.

Laurel stilled, Molly in her arms. "She has to go to the bathroom," she said with a grimace.

"Hurry," Garrett muttered, pointing toward his bedroom. "We can't stay. I wore my uniform and badge tonight. If they saw it, they'll find this place all too easily."

Laurel scurried into his room and Garrett headed to the kitchen. By the time they returned, he'd stuffed a few groceries into a sack. "Let's go."

Gripping his weapon, he led them outside. The door's creak intruded on the night, clashing with the winter quiet. Pale light bathed the yard in shadows. A gust of December wind bit against Garrett's cheeks. A tree limb shuddered.

He scanned the hiding places, but saw no movement, save the wind.

Still, he couldn't guarantee their safety.

"Where are we going?" Laurel asked, her voice low.

Garrett glanced at her, then Molly. "I have an untraceable vehicle lined up. We'll hole up for the night. You need rest. Then after I do a bit of digging, we'll see."

Laurel had brought his past to Trouble. No closing it away again. If his innocent visitors weren't in so much danger, Garrett would have welcomed the excuse to wait it out. His trigger finger itched to face the men responsible for killing his wife and daughter. Except a bullet was too good for them. They needed to die slowly and painfully.

Garrett might have failed to protect his family once, but he wouldn't allow their killer to escape again. He didn't particularly care whether he left the confrontation alive, as long as the traitor ended up in a pine box.

He just prayed he could get these two to safety before the final battle went down.

Laurel stood alone just behind a hedge at the end of the alley, out of sight, squeezing the butt of her weapon in one hand, balancing Molly against her with the other. Garrett had risked crossing those streets to retrieve his vehicle, putting himself in the crosshairs in case the shooters came back.

Every choice he'd made focused on protecting them, not himself. She shivered, but it wasn't the winter chill. She'd made a choice eighteen hundred miles ago to come here. Garrett's immediate response to their arrival had frozen her soul. Now instinct screamed at her to run, to disappear, to try to forget the past and somehow start over.

Maybe she should. He knew what they were up against.

He was worried. Maybe vanishing would be easier. She didn't see Garrett Galloway as a man who would give up easily. But sometimes accepting the reality and moving on was the only way to survive.

A dark SUV pulled into the alley, lights off. Garrett stepped out. "Laurel?" he whispered, searching the hedges with his gaze.

She almost stayed hidden, frozen for a moment. She had some cash. People lived off the grid all the time. So could she.

She could feel his penetrating gaze, compelling her to trust him. What was it about him…?

With a deep, determined breath, she stepped out from behind the hedge. Beads of sap still stuck to her pants from hiding in the firewood pile. The scent of pine flashed her back to memories of camping and fishing and running wild without a care in the world. Her heart broke for Molly. Could Laurel help her niece find that joy after everything that had happened?

Laurel was so far out of her element. She'd taken a leap of faith coming to Trouble and to Garrett, trusting her sister's final words. Her sister had known she was dying; she wouldn't have steered Laurel into danger. Laurel could only pray she had understood Ivy correctly.

She carried Molly to the vehicle. Garrett didn't say anything, but his dark and knowing eyes made Laurel tremble. Did he know she'd almost taken off?

"You decided not to run," he said, opening the door. "I pegged it at a fifty-fifty chance."

He could see right through her. She didn't like it. "I almost did," she admitted. "But I can't let them get away with what they've done." She pushed back a lock of Molly's hair and lifted her gaze to meet his. "Our lives have been turned upside down. Can you help us?"

She didn't usually lay her vulnerabilities out so easily, but this was life and death. She needed his help. They both knew it.

He gave her a sharp nod. "I'll do what I can."

She placed Molly in the backseat and buckled her up. Laurel climbed in beside her. She tucked the little girl against her side. "Where to?"

"I contacted a friend. We need food for a few days. He runs the local motel and does some cooking on the side." Garrett paused. "I don't know how long we'll be on the road. His sister is about your size. I noticed that Molly has a change of clothes, but not you."

Laurel could feel the heat climb up her face at the idea he'd studied her body to determine her size. But he was right. They'd left so quickly, she hadn't had time to do more than purchase a few pairs of underwear at a convenience store. How many men would even think about that?

Garrett didn't turn on the SUV's lights. He drove the backstreets, then pulled up to the side of the Copper Mine Motel behind a huge pine tree, making certain the dark vehicle was out of sight from the road. A huge, barrel-chested man with a sling on one arm eased out of the side door. His wild hair and lip piercing seemed at odds with his neatly trimmed beard, but clearly he'd been on the lookout for them.

Garrett rolled down the passenger-door window. "Thanks, Hondo."

The man stuck his head inside and scanned Laurel and Molly. The little girl's eyes widened when she stared at his arm. "Who drew on you?" she asked.

Hondo chuckled. "A very expensive old geezer, little lady," he said. He placed a large sack on the seat, then a small tote. "You're right, Sheriff. She's about Lucy's size. These clothes are brand-new. Just jeans and some shirts and a few unmentionables." His cheeks flushed a bit.

Laurel scrambled into her pocket and pulled out some bills. "Thank—"

Hondo held up his hand. "No can do." He looked at the sheriff. "If you want them to stay here—"

"After what happened last time, Hondo, I won't let you risk it. Thanks, though." Garrett handed Hondo his badge. "When folks start asking, give this to the mayor."

"Sheriff—"

Laurel clutched the back of the seat, her fingers digging into the leather. She wanted to stop him from giving up his life, but she'd brought trouble to his town. She'd left him with no choice.

"We all have a past, Hondo. Mine just happened to ride in tonight. Something I have to deal with."

Hondo nodded, and Laurel recognized the communication between the two men. The silent words made her heart sink with trepidation.

"Keep an eye on Deputy Keller. He's young and eager, and he needs guidance." Garrett drummed his fingers on the steering wheel. "Come to think of it, you'd make a good sheriff, Hondo. You've got the skills."

"Nah." Hondo's expression turned grim. "I won't fire a gun anymore, and I couldn't put up with the mayor. He's a—" Hondo glanced at Molly "—letch and a thief."

"And willing to take a payoff. I should know. It's how I became sheriff."

Hondo's eyebrow shot up. "You still did a good job. Best since I've lived here."

Garrett shrugged and shifted the truck into Drive. "Goodbye, Hondo."

A small woman with wild gray hair shuffled out of the motel, a bandage on her head. "Hondo?" her shaky voice whispered. "Cookies."

Hondo's expression changed from fierce to utter tenderness in seconds. "Now, sis, you're not supposed to be out of bed. You're just out of the hospital." He sent Garrett an apologetic grimace.

"But you said you wanted to give them cookies," she said, holding a bag and giving Hondo a bright smile.

Laurel studied the woman. She seemed so innocent for her age, almost childlike.

The older woman's gaze moved to Garrett and she smiled, a wide, naive grin. "Hi, Sheriff. Hondo made chocolate chip today."

"We can't say no to Hondo's famous cookies, Lucy."

Garrett's smile tensed, and his gaze skirted the streets. Did he see something? Laurel peered through the tinted windows. The roads appeared deserted.

Lucy passed the bag to Hondo. An amazing smell permeated the car through the open window.

Molly pressed forward against her seat belt. "Can I have one, Sheriff Garrett?"

Hondo glanced at Laurel, his gaze seeking permission. She nodded and Hondo pulled a cookie from the bag. "Here you go, little lady."

With eager hands, Molly took the treat. She breathed in deeply, then stuffed almost the entire cookie into her mouth.

Lucy giggled. "She's hungry."

Hondo placed a protective arm around his sister. "They've got to leave, Lucy. Let's go in."

She waved. "'Bye." Hondo led her back into the house, treating her as if she were spun of fragile glass.

Garrett rolled up the window, lights still off. He turned down the street. "She was shot in the head a couple months ago. We didn't think she'd make it."

Laurel wiped several globs of chocolate from Molly's mouth. "You've made a place for yourself in this town." She resettled the sleepy girl against her body. "I'm sorry." What else could she say?

"They'll find someone else. Things will continue just as they did before I came to Trouble."

The muscle at the base of his jaw tensed, but Laurel couldn't tell if he really didn't mind leaving or if something about this small town had worked its way under his skin. She didn't know him well enough to ask, so she kept quiet and studied the route he took. Just in case.

He headed west down one of the side streets almost the entire distance of town.

Laurel couldn't stand the silence any longer. "Where are we going?"

Garrett met her gaze in the mirror. "I'm taking the long way to the preacher's house. The church auxiliary keeps it ready, hoping they can convince a minister to come to Trouble. It's been empty for almost a year."

"We're just hiding across town?"

"Sometimes the best place to hide is in plain sight," Garrett said. "Besides, I want to do a little searching online. See what I can discover about your sister."

"There was never a news report on the car bomb," Laurel said quietly. On the way here, she'd searched frantically at any internet café or library she could. She kept expecting some news story on an investigation, but she'd seen nothing except a clipping about a tragic accident. In fact, they'd simply stated the entire family had perished in a vehicle fire.

She hugged Molly closer.

They'd lied.

"That tells us a lot." Garrett stopped in the driveway of a dark house, jumped out and hit a code on a small keypad. The garage door rose.

"Small towns," he said with a smile when he slid back behind the wheel. "I check the house weekly."

"Is it safe?"

"The men who took the shot will assume we're leaving town. I would. And I don't want to be predictable."

He pulled the SUV into the garage. The automatic door whirred down behind them, closing them in. Laurel let out a long breath. She hadn't even realized she'd been holding it.

"We're safe?"

"For the moment," Garrett said, turning in his seat. "We need to talk." His gaze slashed to Molly, leaving the rest of the sentence unsaid. *Alone.*

"I know." Laurel bit her lip. She didn't know much. She'd hoped Garrett would somehow have all the answers, that he could just make this entire situation okay.

It wouldn't be that simple. She clutched Molly closer. Laurel had no idea how they would get out of this situation alive.

THE INKY BLACK of the night sky cloaked Mike Strickland's vehicle. Stars shimmered, but it was the only light save a few streetlights off in the distance. Trouble, Texas, was indeed trouble.

"They couldn't have just vanished." Strickland slammed his fist onto the dash of the pickup he'd commandeered.

He'd switched license plates and idled on the outskirts of town, lights off, in silence. He tapped a number into his cell.

"They come your way?" he barked.

"Nothing," Don Krauss said through the receiver, his voice tense. "There are only two roads into town."

"But a lot of desert surrounding it," Strickland muttered in response to his partner's bad news. "We need satellite eyes."

Krauss let out a low whistle. "You request it, the boss'll wonder why."

Strickland activated his tablet computer. The eerie glow lit the cab. "You see the history on this sheriff? Garrett Galloway?"

"Yeah," Krauss said. "So?"

"It's perfect."

"What do you mean?"

"I mean, his backstory is perfect. He grew up in Texas. Went to school at Texas A&M. Joined the corps there. Got a few speeding tickets. Headed to a small town, ran for sheriff."

"Like a thousand other Texas sheriffs."

"Everybody's got something. No late taxes, no real trouble. It feels wrong," Strickland said quietly.

Silence permeated the phone. "What are you thinking?"

"You saw his moves. He didn't learn those in college. Maybe Laurel McCallister didn't get here by chance. Who comes this close to nowhere on a whim?" Strickland glanced around. "And we're at the frickin' end of the earth."

"Still doesn't help to explain if the boss asks about using the satellite."

"I'll say it's a hunch."

Strickland could almost see his partner's indecision. "You gotta learn to take risks, Krauss. If we don't get rid of those two, we're dead. But if my hunch is right, and Garrett Galloway isn't just some hick sheriff, we might be able to feed the boss something new."

"And save our skin. I like it."

"Keep digging on Galloway. Even the best slip up sometimes."

"I'm on it. What do we do until then?"

"I'm contacting headquarters. I want to see a sweep of this part of Texas from the time we arrived until now. This place is dead at night. I want to know who's been moving around and which way they went."

"This could go to hell real fast, Mike."

Strickland scratched his palm. "We just need one break, Krauss. One opening, and our targets won't live long enough to disappear again."

A DIM LIGHT illuminated the preacher's garage. A plethora of boxes provided too many invisible corners and a variety of spooky shadows along the walls. Laurel shivered, but slid out of the car anyway. She bundled Molly into her arms before following Garrett into the preacher's house. He carted in the supplies while she scanned the kitchen, studying each corner, each potential hiding place, each possible weapon. One thing she'd learned in her job: details mattered.

Laurel stepped into the living room. A front door and a sliding glass back door. Not exactly secure. And, of course, doilies everywhere.

The muscles in her shoulders bunched and she cocked her hip. Molly grew heavier and heavier with each movement. She walked back into the kitchen. The decor erupted with grapes and ivy.

So very different from Garrett's house. She'd seen enough of the place to know it hadn't been a home to him, just a way station.

With a sigh, she sat down at the table, shuffling Molly in her lap. She and Garrett needed to talk, but not with Miss Big Ears listening to every word. Molly let out a small yawn. The girl had to be exhausted, but she wouldn't be easy to put down. Even then, the nightmares came all too easily. "Do you have any milk?"

"Warm?" he asked, searching through a couple of cabinets. He pulled out a small saucepan before Laurel could answer.

She nodded. Molly sat up and rubbed her eyes, a stubborn pout on her lip. "I don't want milk. This isn't home. I want my mommy and daddy. I want Matthew and Michaela."

Laurel froze. Molly hadn't mentioned her brother's and sister's names since they'd left Arlington. She blinked quickly and cleared her throat. "I want them, too, honey. But we have to hide. Like a game."

"I don't like this game. You're mean."

The girl's lower lip stuck out even farther and her countenance went from stubborn to mutinous. She crossed her arms, and all Laurel could see in her niece's face was an enraged Ivy. Some might think she could wait Molly out, but her niece could be as tenacious as…well, as Laurel herself.

"It's late, Molly." Her tone dropped, words firm and short. She didn't want to have another drawn-out adventure getting the little girl to bed. Before the car bombing, it had taken some cajoling, at least two stories and two tiny glasses of water before she could get the child to close her eyes. Now…Molly didn't fall asleep until her poor body simply rebelled. "It's time for bed."

"Then why aren't you having hot milk, too?" Molly scrunched her face and crossed her arms.

Garrett turned around. "We're *all* having warm milk, and I made you a *very* special recipe," he said, adding a dash of sugar and a little vanilla and nutmeg to the cups he held.

He set a plastic cup in front of Molly and a glass mug in front of Laurel, then brought over a plate of vanilla wafers. The aroma mingled in the air around them, and Laurel sighed inside. It smelled like home and family. She swallowed briefly, her eyes burning at the corners.

Garrett took a seat, the oak chair creaking under his weight. His large hands rounded the cup. He raised it to his lips, sipped and stared at Molly. She glared back, but when he licked his lips, dunked a vanilla wafer into his cup and bit down, she leaned forward and took a small sip from her cup.

Molly's eyes widened a bit and she tasted more. "Wow. That's yummy. But I want chocolate chip."

"Glad you think so." He slid one of Hondo's cookies toward the little girl and she gifted Garrett with an impish smile.

He winked at Molly, who downed another gulp. Laurel couldn't resist, even though she detested the drink. She chanced a taste. The nutmeg and vanilla hit her tongue with soothing flavors. "Mmm. How'd you come up with this recipe?"

"My wife invented it, actually. Put our daughter to sleep." A shadow crossed his face, then vanished just as quickly. "They're gone now."

"My mommy and daddy and brother and sister are gone, too," Molly said with a small yawn. "I hope they come back soon."

Laurel bit her lip to keep the sob from rising in her throat. "Is there someplace I can settle her down?"

Molly's body sagged against Laurel. A few more minutes and the little girl wouldn't be able to fight sleep any longer.

"Pick a room," Garrett said. "I'll check the perimeter and secure the house."

He strode toward the door.

"Garrett," she said, her voice barely above a whisper. "Thank you. For everything."

"Don't thank me yet, Laurel. Thank me when this is over. Until then, I may just be the worst person you could have come to for help."

GARRETT STOOD SILENTLY in the kitchen doorway as Laurel padded into the living room.

"She asleep?"

Laurel whirled around. Then her head bowed as if it were too heavy for her shoulders. He could see the fatigue in her eyes, the utter exhaustion in every step.

"She was bushed. It's been a rough few days. She just downed the last of her medicine, so hopefully the strep throat is gone."

He tilted his head toward the sofa. "You look ready to collapse. Have a seat. My deputy's been busy tonight calming the town. He received a report of an SUV speeding out of town early tonight. I told him to keep out of sight but watch for it. If they're smart, they'll dump the vehicle."

"But they won't give up," Laurel said.

"I doubt it."

Laurel lowered herself to one end of the sofa, twisting her hands on her lap. "You work for the agency? With my father?"

Garrett sat in the chair opposite her. "In a way." No need to volunteer that he was off the roll. If the agency didn't think he was dead, he'd probably be awaiting execution for treason.

Just one of many reasons he shouldn't allow himself to get too close to Laurel.

But even as he faced her, he felt the pull, the draw. And not because she was gorgeous, which she was, even with that horrible haircut and dye job. Beauty could make him take notice just like any man, but that didn't turn him on half as much as how she'd fallen on top of Molly to protect her.

She was a fighter—a very good thing. She'd have to be for them to get out of this mess alive.

Which put her off-limits. That and the fact that she was James's daughter.

"Your father trained me," Garrett said, trying not to let himself get lost in his attraction for her. "He saved my life, actually."

Laurel tucked her legs beneath her. "I thought it had to be something like that. I used to watch Dad train in the basement when I was a kid. I recognized that move when you dived to the ground." She rubbed her arms as if to ward off a chill. "Ivy worked every night to perfect it. In spite of Dad."

"I heard about the destruction to his office. I don't think James wanted her to join up."

"He was furious, but Ivy has…*had*," she corrected herself, "a mind of her own." Her voice caught and her hands gripped her pants, clawing at the material. "Dad raised us to be independent. She wanted more than anything to follow in Dad's footsteps. She wanted to make the world safe."

Laurel's knuckles whitened and she averted her gaze from his. Every movement screamed at him not to push. Garrett could tell she was barely holding it together, and if she'd given him the slightest indication he would have crossed the room and pulled her into his arms and held her. Instead, he leaned forward, his elbows on his knees, studying her closely. He hated to ask more but he needed information. He had to know. She might not even be aware of the information she possessed. "Where's James, Laurel?"

Her breath shuddered and she cleared her throat. "I don't know. He stopped calling or emailing two months ago. Then out of nowhere a package arrived this week. He sent a charm bracelet to Ivy."

This week. So if James had really sent the package, he'd been alive a week ago. Garrett's shoulders tensed. "Did you bring it?"

Laurel pulled a silver bracelet from her pocket. She touched the small charms and the emotions welled in her eyes. Reluctantly she handed it to him. "Ivy shoved it into my hand as she was leaving that night…" Her voice broke. "She said it was important."

He studied the silver charms. Nothing extraordinary. A wave of disappointment settled over him. Surely there was *something* here. He studied each silver figure, looking for a clue, a message from James. A horse, a dog. A seashell. Several more. Nothing that Garrett understood, but he'd bet Laurel had a story to tell about each one.

The question was, did any of those stories have a hidden message? He handed her back the treasure.

"Tell me about the figures."

She walked through a series of memories. A trip to the ocean with the family right before her mother passed away. Their first dog and his predilection for bounding after fish in freezing mountain streams just to shake off and soak everyone. A horse ride that ended in a chase through a meadow. Her voice shook more with each memory, but the hurt didn't provide anything new. Garrett couldn't see a connection.

He let out a long, slow breath. He had to ask. "How did Ivy die?"

Laurel stared down at the floor. He knew exactly how she felt. Sometimes even looking at another human being could let loose the tears. After Lisa and Ella, he hadn't allowed himself to give in to his emotions. He'd shoved the agony away, buried it in that corner of his mind where it wouldn't bring him to his knees. Garrett had focused on revenge instead. He'd had to in order to survive.

But since Laurel had landed underneath him on the streets of Trouble, the pain he'd hidden had begun scraping at him, digging itself out.

She didn't look up. She simply twisted the denim fabric in her fists. "The explosion burned Ivy almost beyond recognition. She lived. She gave me your name. Then they shot her in the head."

Her voice strangely dispassionate, she went through every detail. When she told him about the single cop's arrival, Garrett closed his eyes. At least one law-enforcement officer on the take. Probably more.

Asking for help was out of the question. And with

James AWOL, they were on their own. She knew it. So did Garrett.

Laurel lifted her lashes and silent tears fell down her cheeks. She wouldn't be facing this alone. In a heartbeat, Garrett knelt at her feet. He pulled her into his arms and just hugged her close.

She clung to him with a desperation he understood. Her fingers dug into his arms. The tiny tremors racing through her tore at his heart. Laurel's heart was broken, and she had a little girl who needed her to be strong.

Laurel needed him, but his body shook as the memories assaulted him. How many nights had he dreamed of his wife and daughter calling out to him, begging for him to save them? But Laurel's pleas were real, in every look, in every touch as she clung to him.

The similarities between Ivy's death and his wife's and daughter's couldn't be denied. He'd find the culprits this time. They wouldn't get an opportunity to hurt anyone else.

Garrett stroked Laurel's back slowly, but she didn't let him go. Her grip tightened.

His pocket vibrated. With one arm still holding Laurel close, he tilted his phone's screen so he could see it. He blinked once at the number. The country code was too familiar. Afghanistan.

"Hello?" He made his greeting cautious, unidentifiable. This was Sheriff Garrett Galloway's phone and number. No one from Afghanistan should know it. That was a life he'd hidden away.

"Garrett?" A weak voice whispered into his ear. A voice he knew.

"James?"

Laurel froze in his arms.

"Garrett, listen to me. The operation has been compromised. Go to Virginia. Get my daughters to safety. They're in danger."

"James, Laurel is with me. What's going on? Where have you been?"

"Oh, God," James cursed. "Ivy knows too much. You have to get her out of there."

Garrett nearly cracked. He didn't want to tell his old friend the worst news a man could receive. Garrett knew the pain of losing a child. Your heart never recovered.

Laurel snagged the phone away from Garrett. "Daddy?" she shouted.

"Laurel, baby. Don't believe what anyone tells you," James said, his voice hoarse. "Promise."

Shouts in Arabic reverberated through the phone. "Find him!"

"Laurel," James panted. "Remember. Ivy's favorite toy."

A spray of gunfire exploded through the speaker.

The phone went silent.

Chapter Three

The phone slipped from Laurel's hand. Her father couldn't be gone. "Daddy?" Her knees gave way and she slid to the floor. She looked up to Garrett. "Get my father back, please."

Garrett scooped up the phone and pocketed it. "I'm sorry. I can't."

He slid his arms beneath her and lifted her. Laurel grasped at him. Her mind had gone numb. She couldn't feel a thing.

With silent steps he carried her to the sofa and sat down on the smooth leather, anchoring her beside him. "Laurel." He used a finger to force her to meet his gaze. "Stay with me, honey."

Her body shuddered, and she couldn't stop the trembling. This couldn't be happening. She wanted to bury herself in Garrett's arms and just forget everything. Pretend the past few days hadn't happened. But she couldn't.

Molly. Molly needed her.

She fisted the material of her jeans, fighting to calm the quake that threatened to overtake her. She had to know. Slowly she lifted her gaze to meet his. "My father? H-he's dead, isn't he?"

Laurel hated the words coming out of her mouth. The

last bit of childish hope, that her father would rescue her and Molly, disintegrated into a million tiny pieces.

Garrett's face resembled a stone statue. He gave nothing away from his expression. He didn't have to say anything.

A burning crept behind her eyes and she pressed the heels of her hands against them, trying to curtain the emotions. "God."

James McCallister had always been invincible. But after the past few months, when she and Ivy had been braced for the worst, for a few brief moments tonight Laurel had gotten her father back.

Now she'd lost him again. Maybe for good this time.

"So many bullets flying," she said, her voice hushed. "How could he possibly survive?"

He hugged her close. "James is smart. And resourceful. If anyone can survive out there, your father can. Right now, I'm more worried about you."

Garrett pulled a small leather case from his pocket and unzipped it before grabbing a small screwdriver. He pulled his cell from his pocket and opened the phone. Quickly, he popped the battery and a small chip from the device and tossed it onto the coffee table before tucking his kit back in his jacket.

"You removed the GPS." The truth hit her with the force of a fist to the chest. "If they're tracing his calls, they know our location. That's what I do for the CIA. Track locations from cell towers and satellites."

"Then you know we can't stay here." Garrett stood.

Laurel swiped at the few tears that had escaped. "How long do we have?" She wasn't stupid. She made her living analyzing data. A price came with being connected at all times. Cell phones, computers, tablets, internet—everyone left a trail. She rose from the couch, her body slightly chilled once she left the warmth of his. She shouldn't get used to it. She knew better. "I'll get Molly."

At her turn, Garrett touched her arm, stopping her. "I'll see you through this."

Laurel paused. "I've driven clear across the country, and a phone call from Afghanistan is bringing whoever killed my family down on top of us…and you. How can it ever be all right? How can I ever keep Molly safe?"

The question repeated over and over in her mind. She knew better than most people how easy it was to track virtually anyone down. Biting her lip, she hurried into the bedroom and wrapped the blankets around Molly. There was no telling where they'd end up.

Molly squirmed a bit. "Aunt Laurel?" she whispered.

"Go back to sleep, Molly Magoo."

"I had a bad, bad dream," she said.

"I've got you," Laurel whispered. "I won't let you go." She hugged Molly tight, humming a few bars of "Hush, Little Baby." Thankfully, Molly snuggled closer, yawned and settled back to sleep.

Laurel exited the bedroom, hurrying to the garage door. It squeaked and she paused, praying Molly wouldn't wake up.

Her niece didn't budge. The dim garage light shone down. Garrett shoved a few last boxes into the back of his SUV and opened the back door, a tender expression when he looked at the sleeping girl in Laurel's arms pushing aside the intensity of just a moment ago. "You better do it. Better if she sleeps."

Laurel gently settled Molly onto the backseat, snapping the seat belt around her.

Garrett closed the door, his movements almost too quiet to hear. "Watch her. I'm going to wipe the house down."

Laurel gave him a quick nod and he disappeared into the house. When he returned, he stuffed a microfiber cloth into his jacket pocket, hit the garage-door opener and slid into the SUV beside her. "Fingerprints would make it too easy for them," he said. "You're on file with the FBI because of your clearance, and so am I."

With a quick turn of the key in the truck, the engine purred to life. He quickly doused the automatic lights and pulled out slowly.

After pressing the outside code, the garage door slid down. The house appeared vacant again.

Laurel looked through the windshield, right, then left, then behind. Tension shivered between them.

Garrett maneuvered onto the deserted street, still without headlights. Trouble had gone to sleep. He didn't plan on anyone waking up as they left town.

He didn't need lights to see anyway. The church auxiliary had gone and wrapped every lamppost and streetlight with garland and twinkle lights, ribbon and tinsel. With each gust of wind the decorations clattered against metal, leaving his neck tense and his hair standing on end.

He gripped the steering wheel, his knuckles whitening. God, he hated Christmas. Hated the memories it evoked. But at least the bulbs lit their way through Trouble.

"Where are we going?" Laurel asked, still alert and searching the surrounding landscape for anything out of the ordinary.

"The middle of nowhere," Garrett said. "Even though some consider Trouble just this side of nowhere."

The vehicle left the city limits, only a black expanse in front of them. This part of West Texas could seem like the end of the world at night, the only light the moon and stars above.

"They'll keep looking for us," Laurel said. "They want us dead."

"No question." Garrett watched the rearview mirror, but no lights pierced the black Texas night. So far, so good.

Laurel shifted in her seat beside him, peering out the front windshield. "It's so—"

"Dark?" Garrett finished.

She glanced over at him, her face barely visible from the light of the dashboard dials. "I've never seen the sky so black."

"When I first moved here from the East Coast, I couldn't get over how bright the stars shone or how dark the countryside could be."

"You didn't grow up around here?"

Garrett quirked a smile. "I was an army brat. I'm from everywhere, but we were never stationed in Texas."

Laurel's eyebrow quirked up. "I'd have taken you for a Texas cowboy."

"I was for a while."

But not anymore.

Garrett focused on the white lines of the road reflecting in the moonlight. No lights for miles around. The tension in his back eased a bit. They were alone.

"It's spooky," Laurel said, her voice barely a whisper. "No sign of civilization."

"You lived on the East Coast all your life?" he asked.

"Dad's job has always been headquartered in D.C. He'd leave town…" Her voice choked. "Someone has to know where he was," she said.

Garrett had been mulling that over. James had been his sole contact since Garrett's attack. He had no backup. No one he could trust.

"What about Fiona?" Laurel's voice broke through the night.

"You know about her?"

"I'm not supposed to. Dad tried to keep his personal life separate, but a few years ago, we caught them at a restaurant. They looked really happy. I'm surprised he hasn't married her. From what we figured out, he's dated her for at least five years."

"More like six," Garrett said. "Though I'm surprised he took her out into public. They work together. That was a huge risk." He drummed his fingers on the steering wheel. "Fiona might be the only person we can trust. She could get at his travel records."

"She could get him backup." Laurel flipped open a cell phone. "He needs help."

"What are you doing?"

"It's prepaid," she said. "I'm not stupid."

Garrett snatched the phone from her. "Not from here. I have equipment we can use to call her. It's more secure. For both of us. We don't want to place her in danger either."

"Dad needs help now."

"James either made it out of that situation alive and is hiding, or there's nothing we can do to help him."

A small gasp escaped from her. Garrett cursed himself, lowering his voice. "Look, I don't mean to be callous, but your dad wanted you safe. That meant more to him than his life or he wouldn't have called. We have to be careful, Laurel. We're alone in this right now, and we have to choose our allies carefully. One slipup…" He let the words go unsaid.

One mistake and they'd finish the job on him and Laurel and Molly would vanish without a trace.

"I understand," she said finally, her voice thick with emotion. "I don't have to like it." She twisted in her seat. "So, this place we're going… How'd you get a secure system?"

"Your dad set it up while I was…incapacitated."

Almost dead.

A small dirt road loomed at the right. Garrett passed it by, drove another ten miles, then pulled off onto a county road heading toward a mine.

"Are we getting close?"

"As close as things get in West Texas," Garrett said. He turned off the lights and the motor. The residual heat would keep them warm for a while.

"We're stopping? We're not that far from town."

Garrett leaned back in his seat and turned his head. "We're waiting. If your tail followed, they should show up soon enough."

Thirty minutes later, the air in the vehicle had chilled. Molly whined in the backseat, wrapping the blanket tighter around her. Garrett cast one last look down the desolate road, then turned the key, and the engine purred to life. He pulled onto the highway, heading back in the direction they'd come.

"You're cautious," Laurel said.

"I'm alive when I shouldn't be." Words more true than he could ever articulate.

"*Who* are you? Really." She shifted and moonlight

illuminated her suspicious expression. "Why did Ivy send me to you?"

The tires vibrated over the blacktop. Garrett refused to let the question distract him. The men following her were good, and he couldn't risk them being seen. Besides, he couldn't tell her. He knew James wouldn't have mentioned his new identity, and if Garrett revealed his previous name, she'd recognize it. As a traitor and a spy.

James had given testimony about Garrett's many infractions. The world had believed the agency's statements. Congress and the covert community trusted James McCallister. Without fail. He might not be a man the public would ever recognize, but in the intelligence community, James McCallister was a legend. The man's lies had saved Garrett's life. And made it so he could never go back. Not unless he wanted a target on his back.

Laurel would have every right to run once she learned the truth, but he couldn't allow that. James's call had done more than warn them. James had risked Garrett's life—and his own—to save the McCallister family. Garrett wouldn't let him down. He owed James too much. He owed the men who had killed his wife and daughter, Laurel's sister and her family—and maybe James—justice. Not courtroom justice, though. The kind that couldn't be bought or bargained for.

"Let's call me a friend and leave it at that," Garrett finally said. "A friend who will try to keep you safe."

"A friend," Laurel mused. "Why doesn't your comment engender me with faith?"

Garrett gripped the steering wheel tight.

"You came to me, Laurel."

"And if I had a choice, I wouldn't be putting our lives in the hands of someone I don't know if I can trust to keep us alive. I like to have all the facts, all the data. You don't add up, Sheriff Garrett Galloway. And that makes me nervous."

What could he say? Her words thrust a sword into his heart. He hadn't been good enough to protect his family. He hadn't seen the true risks when he'd followed up on a small leak at the agency. That one thread had led to their deaths.

Within minutes, the small dirt road appeared. He veered the SUV onto it, the narrow lanes barely visible. The farther they drove in, the bumpier it got. And the more the tension in his chest eased.

Soon they'd started a climb into the Guadalupe Mountains. Leafless branches scraped the sides of the vehicle. Before too long an outcropping of rock blocked their way.

Relieved that the county hadn't seen fit to clear the debris off the glorified cow path, Garrett backed the vehicle into a small clearing. Branches closed over the windshield, barricading them in.

With a sigh he shoved the gear into Park.

"Waiting again?" Laurel asked. "I can't imagine anyone would follow us here."

"The rest of the way to the cattle ranch is on foot. I didn't want the place to be too easy to find."

"I'm known for my sense of direction and I studied the terrain, but even I'm not sure I could find my way here."

"That was the point of buying it," Garrett said. He pressed a button on his watch and the face lit up. "Several hours until daylight. To dangerous to go by foot. One wrong move and we step into nothing and down a two-hundred-foot drop." He reached behind his seat and pulled out a blanket and pillow, thrusting them at her. "Get some rest. When the sun comes up, we'll hike the rest of the way."

"We'll start the search for my father tomorrow?" she pressed, taking the pillow and holding it close to her chest. "I can help. I have my own contacts."

He nodded, but he had his doubts. Laurel might be a gifted analyst, but the moment they ran a few searches, whoever was behind this would start backtracking. Garrett might not know the names of the traitors, but he knew a few dollar amounts. It was in the billions. Too much money was involved for them not to be tracking. Loyalty shouldn't be for sale, but it was.

Which was why Ivy was dead.

Damn it. Garrett should have come out of hiding sooner. He shouldn't have listened to James. He'd wanted to believe his old mentor was close. He'd wanted to believe justice was in their grasp.

"Try to sleep," he said. "Light will come soon."

Laurel snuggled down under the blanket. Garrett shifted his seat back a bit. He'd slept in far worse places.

His hand reached for his weapon. He had to find a way to end this thing. Not only for his family, but before Laurel and Molly paid the price their family had.

The question was how.

James had obviously slipped up.

Garrett couldn't afford to.

A small sigh of sleep escaped from the woman beside him. He tilted his head toward Laurel.

Her blue eyes blinked at him.

"Are we going to get out of this alive?" she whispered. "Truth."

"I don't know."

THE CHRISTMAS LIGHTS decorating every damn corner in Trouble, Texas, twinkled with irritating randomness. Strickland's eye twitched. He leaned forward toward the steering wheel as far as he could and still maneuver the vehicle.

He passed by the sheriff's house for the fifteenth time. Still dark, still deserted.

Headlights illuminated a house ahead.

Strickland whipped the steering wheel and turned down a side street to avoid the deputy crawling all over town. He plowed through a mailbox. With a curse he righted the car.

"Face it," Krauss said, propping his leather work shoe against the dash. "We lost them."

"We can't," Strickland muttered. "She has to die. Her and the kid."

He made his way to Main and pressed the gas pedal. Trouble was a dead end. The SUV shot ahead. The deserted streets of the small town slipped past. They headed into the eerie pitch blackness of the desert without headlights to light the way.

"We have to tell the boss that the McCallister woman is alive, Mike. There's no way we can keep it a secret."

"We still have another day or two," Strickland argued, a bead of sweat forming on his brow. Just the thought made his chest hurt. His pulse picked up speed. He knew what the boss would do. What had been done to others.

"Too risky. If we come clean—"

"We're dead."

Strickland's phone rang.

He yanked the steering wheel and nearly drove off the road. Cursing, he straightened the vehicle.

The glowing screen on the phone turned into a beacon in the night.

Krauss shoved it at Strickland. "It's the boss."

"How—?" He pressed the call button. "Strickland." He forced his voice to sound confident, arrogant.

"The car made the papers," his boss said. "The coroner believes the family died. Well done."

"Thank you." A shiver tickled the back of his neck, as if a black-widow spider had crawled up the base of his skull.

"I have another job for you. It's important."

A string of curses flooded through Strickland's brain. Another job. He had to finish this one first. He couldn't leave it undone. "Of course."

"Two years ago. Another car bomb. Another family. You were in charge."

Strickland remembered it well. No mistakes that time. He'd earned the boss's trust on that job.

"Our target is alive."

Strickland slammed the brakes. The car skidded to a halt. "What?"

"You told me he was dead."

"He wasn't breathing. No way he could have survived those burns." Strickland pulled at his hair. God, a mistake. No. He jumped out of the SUV and paced the pavement. His hand shook as he gripped the phone. Mistakes weren't tolerated. Ever.

"Well, he did. I'm taking care of that loose end. I want you to finish the job. Make certain this time."

Strickland turned on his heel and glared at the twinkling lights of Trouble. He was so screwed. "I'll find him. You can count on me."

"We'll see."

His heart thudded against his chest; his stomach rolled. Bile burned his throat.

"I'll search for him. He can't hide."

"He's not living under his real name."

Krauss rounded the vehicle. Maybe they could split up. It was the only way either man would make it off this assignment alive.

"How do I find him?"

"Your target is Sheriff Garrett Galloway. Trouble, Texas. Kill him this time, Strickland. Be very sure he's dead."

Strickland met Krauss's wide-eyed gaze. He'd heard the words. His partner shook his head in disbelief.

"Oh, and, Strickland? This is your last chance. One more less-than-adequate performance and you'll pray your life will end well before I allow it."

A SLIVER OF SUN peeked over the horizon, the light pricking Laurel awake. She blinked. The muted blue of the winter sky through the windshield brightened with each passing moment. Her cheek pressed against the leather seat. Awareness of the past week washed over her, drowning her in grief.

Ivy, her family. Her father.

Molly.

She jerked her head to one side, then the other, her gaze finally resting on Molly's sweet face.

"She's hasn't stirred," Garrett whispered, his voice low and husky.

Laurel longed to reach out and cuddle her niece, to touch her, to be certain. Molly's pink cheeks were just visible at the edge of the blanket; a small frown tugged at her mouth.

"No nightmares?" Laurel asked, shifting in her seat, combing her hair back from her face with her fingers.

"A few whimpers in the middle of the night. She's obviously exhausted."

"She can't wrap her mind around what happened." Laurel avoided Garrett's sympathetic gaze. She pretended to study the rugged bark of the piñon branches rapping gently against the window. "I can't understand most of the time."

He said nothing, and for that she was thankful. What could he say?

She sent him a sidelong glance. She'd avoided thinking about him as a man, but now, in the close proximity, she couldn't deny her heart stuttered a bit when she looked at him. He was handsome, but that wasn't what drew her. The hard line of his jaw, the determination in his eyes. And his gentleness with Molly. He was the kind of man she could fall for.

Smart, driven and deadly, but with a kind soul. And a heart.

She wanted to reach out and touch him. Just once. She blinked, staring at him. His gaze had narrowed, an awareness in his eyes.

He felt it, too.

The next moment, she wondered if she'd imagined the spark between them. He blinked; the heat doused.

Garrett pulled her SIG from below the seat. "You have extra ammo?"

"Of course," she said. "In my duffel. Dad trained me to go everywhere prepared."

"Not to mention the agency."

"They weren't as tough as my father."

A small grin tugged at the edge of Garrett's mouth.

"So true. I'm going to check out the ranch house. If I'm not back in one hour, I want you to leave." He handed her the keys and a slip of paper. "Contact Daniel Adams. He's the only other person I know who can get you the kind of help you need."

She pocketed the number and clutched the butt of the SIG.

"I'll be back," he said, opening the door.

"Be careful."

He tipped the brim of his Stetson before closing the door softly.

His catlike moves revealed more training than Laurel had. He disappeared around a pile of rocks. She caught a glimpse of his hat for a moment, but within minutes he'd vanished.

She clutched the keys in her hand. She had a full tank of gas, Molly in the backseat. She could run, just disappear.

Forget the past?

The fiery inferno of her sister's car burned the backs of her eyelids. Where was the justice in disappearing?

Her sister never would have let it go. Laurel dug into her pocket and pulled out the prepaid cell. No signal. If anything did happen, how would she find help? Her father wouldn't appreciate it if she put Fiona at risk.

Who could Laurel ask?

There was a reason she'd traveled all the way across the country. She had no choice but to trust Garrett. Him and his secrets.

Her father had called Ivy the judge and jury and Laurel a lie detector. Perhaps it was true. If she had enough information, Laurel could usually figure out the truth. It was what made her good at her job.

As long as the information was solid.

And with Garrett, she had nothing.

Laurel wrapped her arms around her knees, the gun heavy in her hand, comforting in its power. The chill of the winter air outside seeped into the car. She tugged the blanket closer and glanced at the clock. Thirty minutes. And he wasn't back.

A gust hit the tree, scraping the side of the truck. She tensed, gripping the butt of her SIG even tighter.

Forty-five minutes.

Laurel eyed the keys she'd placed on the dash. Fifteen minutes left.

A loud yawn sounded from the backseat. "Where are we?" Molly sat up. "Cars aren't for sleeping." She looked outside, and her eyes widened. "We're in the woods."

Laurel twisted in her seat and faced her niece with a forced smile on her face. "Like the three bears."

Molly gave her aunt a skeptical, you-can't-be-serious expression.

"Look!" Molly squealed, pointing out the window.

Laurel brought the gun to the ready and aimed at the window.

Garrett paused in his tracks and raised his hands with an arched brow.

Molly giggled. "Sheriff Garrett is a good guy. You can't shoot him."

Laurel dropped the weapon and stuffed it into her jacket.

With a forced smile on his face, he opened the back door. "And how is Sleeping Beauty this morning?"

"Hungry," Molly said, rubbing her eyes.

"I think we can take care of that. But first we're going

for a little walk." Garrett met Laurel's gaze and gave her a slight nod. "All clear."

She slipped out of the seat and headed to the back of the truck.

"Don't carry too much," Garrett said. "The terrain is rocky. I'll come back for the rest later." He turned to Molly. "Want to wear my hat?" he asked, holding it out to the small child.

Molly gazed up at him, her blue eyes huge. She nodded and Garrett tipped the hat on her head. It fell over Molly's eyes and she giggled. "It's too big."

"Are you saying I have a big head, young lady?" Garrett asked with a smile, his eyes twinkling.

Molly's grin widened and for the first time in days she lost that haunted look in her eyes. "Bigger than mine," she said. "You're funny. I like you, Sheriff Garrett."

"I like you, too, sugar."

The endearment made Molly smile again, but a swallow caught in Laurel's throat, because the normalcy wouldn't last. It couldn't.

Garrett led them through the jagged mountains, so unlike the woods in Virginia. Craggy rocks, the evergreen of piñon trees, lower to the ground, searching for water. Dry and harsh. Laurel stumbled and fell against a rock, scraping her hand.

Garrett was right beside her in an instant, helping her to her feet, his arm firm around her waist. His touch lingered for a moment, as did the concern in his brown eyes. "You okay? It's not much farther."

Molly stood, holding her lion against her chest. The little scamp hopped from one rock to the next.

"Fine," Laurel said, but her belly had started to ache. It always did when the nerves were uncontrollable. Every moment buried the truth further. They were truly out in the middle of nowhere. Without communication, without anyone but Garrett. How long could it last? How long would they be here?

How could they help her father from here? Much less themselves?

The questions whirled through her mind until a small stone-and-wood structure jutted from an incline.

The ranch house, with a porch surrounding it, wasn't large. Off to the side a small corral appeared more abandoned than anything. She couldn't see any sign of livestock.

"Here we are," he said, climbing up the steps and opening the door. He opened a panel and entered a code. Laurel raised an eyebrow.

"Sensors around the perimeter."

She nodded just as Molly raced in. The little girl's vibrating energy circled the room. She ran from the couch to a nightstand, finally bending down to poke at the fireplace screen. Rocks climbed ceiling to floor, the structure dominating the small living room.

Garrett set a bag in the simple kitchen on one wall.

"Put your things in here." He pushed into a small room with a double bed, chest of drawers and nightstand. No photos, no pictures on the wall. Plain, simple and utilitarian.

"The bathroom is through there," he added. "Just a shower and toilet."

"Is this your bed?" Laurel set down her duffel. "It's fine, but where will you sleep?"

Garrett hesitated. He glanced down at Molly. "Which side of the bed do you want, sugar?"

Molly grinned. "*I'm* gonna sleep in that big bed?" She

ran over and bounced on the side. "When my brother and sister get here, all three of us can fit."

Laurel averted her gaze from Molly, landing on Garrett. A glimmer of sympathy laced his expression.

"I'm going to show your aunt Laurel something. Okay?"

Molly nodded, hugged her lion and started a conversation with the beast.

Laurel took one last look at Molly and followed Garrett into the great room. "I don't know how to explain it to her."

He rubbed the stubble on his chin. "It won't be easy, but she has you. Molly will be okay, eventually. There's going to be a fall when she recognizes that her family is gone. Believe me, I know."

Laurel stilled and took in Garrett's features. Strain lined his eyes and a darkness had settled over his face. She reached out her hand and touched his arm. "I can see that."

He looked down at her hand touching him. "I'll show you my setup here. You may need it."

A step away had her clutching at air. He'd fled her touch. She didn't know why she'd reached out to him, but something in his expression called to her, made her want to comfort him, even as her own heart was breaking.

He unlocked the door leading into the second room in the cabin. She gasped. High-tech equipment she recognized from her job at the CIA lined two walls. Monitoring equipment—a secure phone and a very top secret computer system. A world map hung on one wall. Several pegs dotted some of the more sensitive countries. Below the map, a cot with a pillow and a rumpled blanket seemed to speak volumes.

The bedroom he'd given to her and Molly wasn't where he slept. When he visited this ranch house, he slept here.

"And I was worried I didn't have cell service," she said. "You could contact anyone anywhere in the world from here."

"Hand me your phone," Garrett said.

"It's powered off." She handed it to him.

"Good. They shouldn't be able to trace it to you since it's prepaid, but we can't afford to take chances. It still pings a cell tower." He removed the battery and GPS chip. "Pop in the battery if you have to use it," he said, tossing the GPS in the trash.

"You could track my father with this equipment," Laurel said, moving into the room.

"Maybe." Garrett sat down in one of the chairs and nodded his head at Laurel to take the other seat. "You have to understand, I promised James I'd stay out of the investigation. I have. For his sake."

"But—"

Garrett raised his hand to interrupt her argument. "I get it. Things have changed. We're taking a huge risk, though. I could make his situation worse. You have to understand that, Laurel."

How much worse could it get?

Laurel couldn't sit still. She paced back and forth. Her father could already be dead. But if he wasn't, what if this decision caused him to lose his life? Her mind whirled with confusion. The analytical part of her brain didn't like the missing data.

She lifted her gaze to him before taking her seat again. "If your father were missing, what would you do?"

"If my father were still alive, I'd do whatever it took to find him."

"And live with the consequences?"

"In this situation, yes. The alternative is worse," Garrett said. "Your father has made a lot of enemies over the years, but more than that, if we don't discover who is behind your sister's murder, you and Molly will never be safe. Those men will never stop coming after you."

"Oh, a big kitty! Come here, kitty, kitty." Molly's voice rang out from outside the cabin.

Laurel jumped to her feet at the same time as Garrett. "What kind of cats—?"

"Not domestic."

Chapter Four

Garrett pulled the Beretta from its holster and slammed through the front door of the ranch house. Laurel's footsteps thundered behind him.

"Oh, God," she whispered.

Molly stood about ten feet from the porch, across a clearing. Her hand reached out toward a large cougar, its long, thick tail swinging to and fro.

"Good kitty," Molly sang out, stepping forward.

The cat crouched, hissing.

"Molly," Garrett said, his tone firm with what his daughter had called his *mean voice.*

The little girl froze. "I didn't do anything wrong."

He guessed the *mean voice* still worked, but the memory also returned that horrible helplessness that he never experienced when facing his own death—or even the death of another agent.

Only a child's death could evoke the fear that seeped through his very soul.

Without hesitation, Garrett aimed his weapon at the animal, cursing inside for the animal to stop moving. As it was, it was going to be an impossible shot.

"Molly." Garrett forced his voice to remain calm.

"That's not a kitty cat. I need you to stay very, very still, sugar. Don't move. I'm going to shoot a gun."

"Too loud," Molly whimpered, shaking her head back and forth, clasping her ears with her hands and squatting down.

Damn it. She'd made herself a target. The cat hunched down on its front paws, clearly preparing to pounce. Garrett couldn't wait. What he wouldn't give for his father's old Remington. He could take out the animal with one shot. A rifle was so much more accurate than a handgun at this distance.

The cat growled, opening its mouth in a show of aggression.

Molly squealed and tumbled backward, becoming a perfect target for the predator.

Garrett ran at Molly, shouting. He had to get closer. Startled, the animal shifted its focus, turning away from Molly. Garrett took four shots at the mountain lion. The big cat yowled once and bounded away, disappearing into the cover of the trees. He'd aimed the shots wide on purpose. Injuring the animal could have done more harm than good, especially if he hadn't been able to take it down. A wounded cat could tear out Molly's throat in seconds.

He'd played the odds.

Thankfully, the animal hadn't gone against its nature. Garrett kept his weapon on hold, searching beyond the shrubs and piñons for the cougar. Cats were normally reclusive, avoiding humans, but they were curious as well.

"Get her," he called to Laurel.

Behind him, she scooped Molly into her arms. The little girl sobbed. Laurel hugged her niece close. "It's okay. You're safe."

Garrett backed toward them, scanning the perimeter,

but there was no movement beyond the tree line. He kept the Beretta in his hand and headed to the house.

"I—I want my mommy." Molly hiccuped from Laurel's arms. *"Mommy!"*

"It's gone," he said.

No need to take chances, though. Within seconds, he'd escorted them inside. Once they were safe, he shut and locked the door. The little escape artist had figured out the dead bolt. He'd have to secure the door another way. It had been a long time since he'd childproofed anything.

His knees shook slightly, and he grabbed the door-jamb for support. Garrett could face down at AK-47 or an Uzi without increasing his heart rate by a beat or two.

A milk-faced Laurel sank into the sofa, rocking Molly in her arms. The little girl's cries tugged at his heart. Laurel rubbed her niece's back, and she turned her head to Garrett.

Thank you, she mouthed.

He'd brought them here, though. He'd put Molly in danger. He should have anticipated. He knew better. Whoever said girls didn't get into as much trouble as boys hadn't lived with his Ella. Or Molly.

"I just wanted to play with the kitty," she said through hiccups. "He's the same color as my lion."

Now that they were safe, Garrett's breathing slowed from a quick pant. He crouched next to the sofa. "I know, Molly, but that kind of kitty doesn't play. He's a wild animal. No more going outside alone. Okay?"

"I want your promise, Molly," Laurel said, her voice stern. "You can't go outside without me or Sheriff Garrett."

The little girl squirmed in Laurel's arms. "Okay."

Laurel allowed her niece to slide to the ground, but Garrett didn't trust that look. His daughter had played the game before. He held Molly firmly by the shoulders, looking her squarely in the eyes. "Listen to me, Molly. Outside is dangerous. We're in the woods and you could get lost. We might not find you. I want a real promise."

Her lower lip jutted out.

"Molly."

She let out a huge sigh. "I promise. Cross my heart, stick a nail in my eye, even if I don't want to."

Garrett held on to a chuckle at the little girl's mutilation of the saying. He stuck out his hand. "Deal."

She straightened up and placed her small hand in his. "Deal. Can I have something to eat? I'm hungry."

Kids. Hopefully she'd been scared enough to mind him. Mulling over how he could keep Molly in the cabin, Garrett walked over to the bag of food on the table.

"Play with your stuffed lion, Molly. We'll let you know when breakfast is ready."

"His name is Hairy Houdini. Daddy named him after me 'cause I always disappear." She ran off to the other room, swinging the lion in the air as if he were flying.

Laurel staggered to the kitchen table and slumped in the chair. She held her head in her hands. "Oh, God."

"You okay?" Garrett asked after pulling a skillet from a cabinet and setting it on the stove.

"My niece was almost a midmorning snack for a mountain lion. Not really."

"She's something else."

Laurel looked at the bedroom door. The little girl had an animated discussion going on with her toy. "Like nothing happened. Is that normal?"

"Kids are more resilient than we are," Garrett said before he could stop himself.

"You've had experience." Laurel folded her hands together. Quiet settled in the room, with only Molly's chatter breaking through.

Garrett's teeth gritted together. He wasn't having this conversation. She didn't need to know how he'd failed to protect his own wife and daughter. Not when he needed her to trust him.

So why did silence feel like a lie? "I'll be back in a few minutes," he said. "I need to get the rest of our supplies." He hurried out the door without giving her time to quiz him.

Idiot. The winter chill bit through his bomber jacket. He scrambled over the rocks and made it to the SUV in record time. He was giving too much away. What was it about her that made Laurel feel so...comfortable? He couldn't afford to like her. Emotions had no place in his world right now. Not when he was fighting an enemy that held all the cards.

He had to get back on track.

By the time he returned to the house with the last of the supplies, the crackle of bacon and a heavenly aroma filled the room.

"I found the bacon in the freezer," she said.

Garrett's stomach rumbled. He hadn't eaten since last night. Without saying a word, he set the groceries on the table and started putting them away. They worked side by side, together. Too comfortably. He sliced a couple of loaves of Hondo's homemade bread. Laurel slid one out of his hands, her touch lingering for a moment. She slathered the toast with butter and popped the slices in the broiler.

"After Molly eats, why don't you distract her?" Garrett said, clearing his throat. "I'll do some looking into your father."

Laurel put down a knife and turned slowly toward him. "How long have you been out of the game?" she asked.

"What makes you think—?"

"At first glance I didn't notice," she said, "but I checked out the equipment a second time while you were gone. Most of it is a couple years old. You haven't upgraded. If you were active, you'd have the latest."

"Molly, time to eat," Garrett called out.

He heard the slap of shoes as she raced into the room. She squealed and sat at the table. "Hairy and I are starving to death." She dug into the bacon and toast, munching down.

"Not a topic for conversation. I get it," Laurel said. "So, you have a favorite football team, Garrett?"

He looked over his shoulder and sighed. "Between your job and your father's career, you have to know sharing information is a bad idea."

"Not much choice. My father is in trouble. So am I. You may be able to help us, but you need me. I have contacts. People I trust. If we're careful they won't be able to trace us back here."

"Really? Even on my *outdated* equipment? Did Ivy trust them, too?"

Laurel hissed at the barb, but Garrett didn't waver.

"I won't apologize. Right now it's all about finding your father. And that means finishing the job your sister started. On our own."

MIKE STRICKLAND SAT in the SUV a block down from the sheriff's office. They'd gotten nowhere searching the man's house. The damn town hadn't had one 9-1-1 call the entire night.

He stroked his stubble-lined jaw. He'd been awake all night, knowing if he fell asleep and missed his chance, his life would be worth nothing.

Strickland couldn't believe Garrett Galloway was actually acknowledged traitor Derek Bradley.

Wasn't his fault the man had decided to take his family somewhere that day. Strickland shoved aside the prickle of regret. He'd gained the boss's confidence with that job. And he'd stayed alive.

He'd also attached himself to the organization the boss had created. Selling guns and secrets to the highest bidder: governments, terrorist organizations, corporations—it didn't matter.

Nothing mattered but the dollars. Loyalty didn't mean squat, and the boss didn't suffer fools. The stakes in the game were too high to risk compromise.

Unless Strickland killed Bradley—make that Galloway—before he saw the boss again, he'd be the next example.

A beat-up truck trundled in front of the sheriff's office. A young deputy jumped out of his truck. He turned the doorknob, then paused.

So, the sheriff was usually in before now.

The deputy dug his keys from his pocket, inserted one into the lock and pushed the door open.

Strickland's phone vibrated. "Tell me you have something," he bit out to Krauss.

"Nothing. Checked out the abandoned house where we triangulated the sheriff's cell signal. Evidence of someone there, but gone. No prints."

"His place?"

"Nothing."

"We're out of options," Strickland said. "I'm going to have a chat with the young deputy." He ended the call, tucked his unidentifiable Glock in his holster, waited for a couple of cars to pass by and stepped out of the vehicle.

He crossed the street and slipped into the sheriff's office.

"Deputy?"

"Can I help you, sir?"

The young man poked his head out from the back room. Strickland could take him out now and no one would have a lead to follow. He ran his hand over the weapon. "Looking for the sheriff."

The deputy sighed. "You and me both. He's not here yet."

"When do you expect him back?"

The kid stiffened, finally recognizing Strickland could very well be dangerous. "I told you I don't know. How can I help you?"

The kid shifted his stance, subtly showing his side-arm.

Strickland flashed his identification badge. "Federal business," he commented. "Contact him."

The deputy's face paled. "Of course." He stumbled to the desk and dialed a number. After thirty seconds his face fell. "Sheriff, a federal agent is here. He needs to see you—"

Strickland grabbed the phone. He lifted the receiver and punched in the erase code. "I didn't tell you to leave a message. Can't risk it."

The deputy stood up, his gaze narrowed, suspicious. "Why are you here?"

"Your sheriff might not be who he says he is, Deputy. I'm here to find out exactly who Garrett Galloway is."

"With all due respect, no way, sir. Sheriff Galloway is the real deal."

"You think so, do you? He ever talk about his past? He ever tell you anything about where he came from?"

"Well, no, but still, he's a good sheriff. Everyone says so."

"Maybe now. My agency has reason to believe he's behind a lot of crimes. Under his *real* name. You recognize the name Derek Bradley?"

The kid gasped. "He's a traitor. Sold secrets to terrorists. Caused a lot of men to get killed overseas. He got himself blown up a couple years ago."

"So the public was led to believe."

The deputy shook his head. "Not Sheriff Galloway."

Strickland leaned in. "Does he trust you?"

The kid nodded. "Yeah."

"He wouldn't leave town without letting you know, would he?"

"No, sir."

Strickland patted the kid's cheek. "Okay, then, here's what I want you to do. If he contacts you, I want you to keep your phone on. Don't end the call." He squeezed the deputy's shoulder. "What's your name?"

"Deputy Lance Keller, sir."

"Well, Lance, are you a patriot?"

The kid sprang to attention. "Yes, sir."

"Okay, then. You do this, and your country will thank you."

The deputy met his gaze. "I think you're wrong about the sheriff, sir."

"Could be. If he's innocent, nothing will happen, will it? And you'll have helped clear him."

Keller smiled. "Yes, sir."

"If he's guilty, you've saved a lot of lives."

Strickland turned and opened the front door. "I'm counting on you, Keller."

He walked back to his truck and picked up his phone. "Kid's clueless."

"You kill him?"

"Came a second away from pulling the trigger, but not yet. Galloway's a straight-as-an-arrow spy. It's what got him into trouble in the first place. He might contact the deputy. And if he does, we'll have him." Strickland paused. "*Then* I kill him."

GARRETT PEEKED INTO the living room. Laurel and Molly were playing hide-and-seek, with Hairy Houdini the key player. He smiled softly. It had been so long since he'd heard that kind of joy.

So many lost memories.

And Laurel. She had his heart beating again. He didn't know if he liked feeling again. A cold heart made it easier to focus on revenge.

She let out a laugh and tackled Molly in a gentle hold. Those two had melted the ice encasing his heart. And Laurel had lit a fire.

He wanted to scoop her into his arms, touch her and hold her until she trembled against him. They could both forget the past and lose themselves in each other. He'd recognized the heat, the awareness in her eyes.

She wouldn't say no.

Problem was, Laurel was a forever kind of woman. And Garrett had stopped believing he had a forever.

The reality made this decision easier. He planted himself in his office chair and picked up the secure line. For a moment he hesitated. Daniel Adams had been through hell, but the man had connections...and he was one of the good guys. These days, men who lived by a code of honor were few and far between. Many talked the talk. Few walked the walk.

He punched in the number Daniel had given him.

"Adams." Daniel's voice held suspicion.

Garrett was silent for a few moments. Daniel said nothing either, obviously unwilling to give anything away.

"It's Garrett Galloway," he finally said.

"If you're calling on this line, it must be serious, and not to request an invitation to Christmas dinner."

"You said to call if I needed a favor. I might. And it's a big one. Just how covert can your *friends* be?"

"Very. What's the situation?" Daniel's voice went soft. A few loud squeals sounded in the background before the snick of a door closing muffled the noise.

"My past is raising a dangerous head, complete with teeth. A woman and her niece are in the cross fire. If I fail, they need new identities and a new life. Untraceable, undetectable."

Daniel let out a low whistle. "I always wondered about you, Garrett."

"Look, Daniel, don't run a search on me. Eyes are everywhere. The minute you pull strings, those eyes will come back on you and your friends. You get me?"

"I played the game," Daniel said. "Do your friends know what they're in for if they disappear?"

"I'll make sure they understand. We're not far from

that gorge you hid out in. How long will it take you to get here?"

"I can have a chopper there in less than an hour."

"I think we'll have to talk about that." Behind him Laurel stood in the doorway, foot tapping. "You're palming us off? Where's that idea of working together, *Sheriff*? I'm not ready to give up on having my life back yet."

Daniel chuckled at the other end of the phone. "She reminds me of my wife. Doesn't take any prisoners. You need me, call this number. I'll have the helicopter on standby."

"No details. To anyone."

"None needed. They know me. You had my back once, Garrett. I've got yours."

Garrett hung up the secure phone and turned around in his chair. He'd know very soon which direction this operation would be taking.

He had a feeling he knew. And that Laurel wasn't going to like it.

Noon had come and gone. Laurel kissed Molly's forehead and quietly closed the door to the bedroom. The little girl had fallen asleep before her usual nap time, but she was exhausted. Even though the weather was brisk, the sun had shone. They'd explored outside, careful to make enough noise to startle any other predators from coming too close. They'd collected pinecones. The moment Laurel had crossed the baseball-sized tracks of the big cat, she and Molly had scurried back to the house. She didn't want to come face-to-face with it again, even with her SIG.

She hovered over the sleeping girl for a few minutes. Molly hadn't mentioned her brother or sister all morning. Laurel couldn't help but worry. When the truth hit, it would hit hard.

She left a small crack between the door and the jamb so she could hear Molly if she woke.

Quietly she exited into the living room. Garrett must still be in his office. She padded across the wood floor and stuck her head through the door.

He sat in front of the wall of electronics, bent over, studying the monitor intently. He typed in a few keystrokes. The screen turned red.

He cursed and quickly pressed a button.

"No luck?"

The chair whirled around. He'd removed his hat and his hair stood up, as if he'd run his fingers through it dozens of times.

"They've closed off most of the loopholes I knew about. Not surprised, just irritated. I let James…" His voice trailed off.

She eased through the doorway. "What about my father?"

For a moment it looked as if he wouldn't tell her. Finally he met her gaze. "I kept a low profile. It was the wrong decision."

"I can help," she said. "Let me do my job. What are you looking for?"

He glanced at the cracked-open door. "Molly?"

"Asleep. Her afternoon naps are usually an hour or so, if her visits with me hold."

"Front door locked?" he asked with a raised brow.

"Dead bolted and chained at the top," Laurel said with a shake of her head. "Ivy said Molly started finding ways out of her crib at just a year old. Once she caught her climbing over the side rail and then just hanging there by her fingertips before jumping down and going after her lion."

"Maybe she'll be a gymnast." Garrett chuckled. "Or a spy." His face turned serious. "I'm trying to identify James's last *official* location, but I haven't found a record of travel, much less any files. His data is locked down tight."

He faced the screen and Laurel bent over him. She rested her hand on his shoulder and leaned in. "I monitor data coming from Afghan tribal leaders," Laurel said. "I might have access to some locations or at least chatter."

"Can you get in from the outside?"

"Are you on a classified network?"

"Secure, not classified," Garrett said. "No way I could pull that off for this long without someone noticing."

"I could get at some information." She gnawed at her lip. "I could end up leading them here, Garrett."

"I know."

He rose from his chair and paced the room. "James said the operation had been compromised. That probably means they'll be looking for my signature."

"He also mentioned Ivy's research."

Garrett tapped his temple with his forefinger. "You know your sister. You know how she thinks. Maybe we can get to her files through you, instead of me or James."

"There's still the problem of leading them here. If I use her name or any identifying information, they'll know it's me. Us."

"You're right." He patted the console. "We do much more here and it'll be the last bit of info they need to come after us."

At the look on Garrett's face, Laurel stepped back,

understanding flooding through her. Garrett *had* learned from her father. Classic James McCallister M.O. "You *want* them to catch you?" She grabbed his shirt collar. "You saw what they did to Ivy. You can't do that."

"You're too damned observant." Garrett scowled at her. "And yeah, I know *exactly* what they might do to me. On the other hand, they won't be expecting me to be ready for them. I'm going to let them think they're getting the drop on me. Surprise is worth a lot."

"It's crazy."

"You think I love this plan, Laurel? If I were planning this op, this would be option Z. But that's where we're at. It's the *only* option. We don't have the insider to help us. We don't know who the traitor is. Your father hasn't contacted us again. We have no choice."

"What about Molly?" Laurel whispered.

"I called a friend while I was retrieving the groceries. He's someone I can trust. Maybe the only person I can trust. He has friends who can hide you and Molly while I go after James."

She could see he'd made up his mind, but there had to be another way. She sat across from him and grabbed his hands, squeezing them tight. "Let me try? We can cut off communication if it's taking too long or if I detect someone tracing us." She met his gaze. "I'm good at what I do, Garrett. Let me try."

"I watch every move. The moment there's feedback, we turn it off and go with my plan. Agreed?"

She was silent for a moment.

"Those are my conditions, Laurel."

"Agreed."

She took a seat and stared at the keyboard. She prayed her abilities wouldn't fail her now.

A LOUD SCREAM yanked James McCallister awake. For a split second he didn't know where he was. Then the pain overwhelmed him. He fought not to cry out.

He shifted his legs, trying to ease the tension in his shoulders. His jailer had shoved him into this dirt-walled prison, clamped a manacle over each wrist and whipped him until he lost consciousness.

James had said nothing.

Footsteps walked down the hallway. James looked up; his eyes widened with shock, and then nausea rose up his throat.

He couldn't believe it.

And yet the proof stood before him.

"I...I wouldn't have guessed," he said through dry lips. "You fooled me."

"Of course I did, but you cost me nearly a billion dollars this month, James. I'm not happy. You know I get cranky when I'm not happy."

A knife sliced down his chest, drawing blood. He hissed, pulling away, but the movement only caused droplets to fall to the floor.

"And Garrett Galloway."

James struggled to keep his heart from racing.

"Oh, yes. I know he's alive. You hid him well. I just wanted you to know that I'm smarter than you are." His captor lifted out a small device.

James nearly groaned. Impossible. No one should have discovered his secret.

"That's right. I can track Garrett Galloway anywhere. He's dead, James. And it's all your fault."

Chapter Five

Laurel leaned forward in the chair, staring at the screen. The disappointment nearly suffocated her.

"It's okay," Garrett said softly. His hand rubbed her back.

"I can't find him." She shrank away from his touch. She didn't want comfort. She'd failed. She'd been so certain. She shoved away from the console.

"Don't do this to yourself." He stood beside her and turned her into his arms. He looked down at her. The expression on his face held too much sympathy.

"I failed my father. I failed Ivy. I failed you." She tried to push away, but he refused to let her go. She shook her head. "I failed Molly."

Laurel couldn't stop the tears from rolling down her face. She'd thought she could do this. She'd believed if she were in her element she could save them all. What a fool she'd been.

"Listen to me. These people are good. I wasn't able to catch them. Neither was Ivy. Or your father. You didn't let anyone down."

He pressed her into his chest. She clung to his shirt, gripping him tight. His warmth seeped through her as the sobs racked her body.

"Shh," he muttered. "It's okay."

Laurel couldn't stop the flood of emotions: the guilt, the pain, the grief. Everything overwhelmed her. She didn't know how long she stood in Garrett's embrace, but when she came up for air, her body was spent.

He rubbed her back awhile longer, whispering soft words of comfort—lies, really. Because nothing would be all right. It couldn't be.

Finally she pushed against his chest and tried to hide her face from him. He tilted her chin up. "You don't have to hide. You just did what I wanted to do from the moment I came to Trouble."

With a swipe of her tears, she cleared her throat. "Doesn't do any good. Now I'm exhausted and fuzzy headed."

"And less likely to crumble under the pressure. Molly will need that strength from you."

"You're going to lay down a trail of bread crumbs, aren't you?"

"Yeah."

"Without backup? You can't."

Garrett brushed aside the chopped hair that didn't feel like hers. "I can't let them use you and Molly as leverage. Not against James. Or me." He closed in on her, his large frame looming. His presence sucked the air from the room. He took her hand in his. "You can trust Daniel, and he has connections. If I fail, they can give you a new life."

She gripped his fingers. "Dad will kick my butt if I let you sacrifice yourself without a fight."

"He'd understand," Garrett said, his face certain, frozen like stone.

"Convince me," Laurel said, placing her hand on his chest. "They could end up using you anyway."

Garrett whirled away from her, stalked across the room and shoved his hands through his hair. "You are the most stubborn woman I have ever had the misfortune of meeting. And that's saying a lot given the work I do. Why can't you just agree?"

"Because I can't let you go on a suicide mission." She followed him, reaching up to his shoulders. Something more was going on with him. She could feel it.

She tugged at his arm, trying to see his face, look into his eyes. When he finally faced her, she gasped at the pain in his expression.

"Why are you doing this, really?" she whispered, leaning into him.

"It's not important." Garrett cleared his throat and then his hand trembled. He cupped her cheek. "You and Molly need to be safe. I can't let anything happen to you."

The air grew thick between them.

"Because of your loyalty to my father?"

His thumb stroked her skin. She closed her eyes. Something had been simmering between them since they'd met.

"Because I can't let anyone else I care about get hurt."

With a groan he lowered his mouth to hers. She clung to him, holding his face between her hands while he explored her lips.

He tasted of coffee, a hint of cinnamon and something uniquely Garrett. With each caress of his mouth, a tingle built low in her belly as if he had a direct line to her soul. A low rumble built within his chest and he scooped her against him, flattening her breasts against his chest.

This wasn't like any first kiss she'd ever experienced. He took her mouth as if he owned her, and she met him more than halfway. When he tried to raise his head she tugged him back down.

"More," she whispered. "Make me feel."

She wanted to lose herself in his touch. She tugged his shirt from his pants and let her fingers explore the skin of his belly, then up to the hair on his chest.

"You're playing with fire," he muttered.

"Then let me burn."

A squeaking door erupted between them. Laurel's eyes grew wide.

"Molly."

"Aunt Laurel, I'm bored. There aren't any toys here." Molly shoved into the office, her little arms crossed. Laurel sprang out of Garrett's arms, her face flushed.

"What are you doing?"

Garrett cleared his throat and tried to order his body under control. He glanced down at Laurel. She didn't appear any less flushed. Her cheeks went red and she pulled her hands from beneath his shirt. He regretted the loss, but in some ways Molly had saved them both. He smiled at the little girl. "So, sugar, it's almost lunchtime. How would you like to go on a picnic?"

Laurel stepped back, her expression stunned. "I don't think—"

"What about the big kitty?" Molly asked, her voice tentative.

"Well, I'll be there, and cats usually stay away from people. We'll be fine."

"Absolutely not." Laurel shook her head. "It's December."

"December in West Texas isn't the same as anywhere else," Garrett said. "All she needs is a jacket. And we both need to run off some energy, take in a bit of brisk air." He sent her a pointed glance.

"Oh, please, Aunt Laurel," Molly said, tugging on her shirt. "I wanna have lunch outside and go 'sploring with Sheriff Garrett."

Laurel's face softened, and Garrett could see her indecision. Laurel loved her niece. He liked her fierce protectiveness. Laurel McCallister had a lot of her dad in her. Courage that started with a spine of steel. Courage that made her way too attractive for his peace of mind.

Besides, if they stayed in this cabin, Garrett didn't know how much longer he could resist her. James would take him to the torture chamber if Garrett put the moves on his little girl.

"I need to take a look around and set a few pieces of equipment." Laurel sent him a meaningful gaze. So she'd decided to work with him.

One surprise after another, this woman.

"Yay!" Molly twirled around and around. "We're going on a picnic. We're going on a picnic," she repeated over and over again in a singsong voice.

She skipped around the small cabin.

"Are you sure about this?"

"Do you want to try to keep her inside all day and then get her to sleep tonight?" Garrett arched a brow.

Laurel's gaze fell to Molly's movements, and then she sighed. "I thought she'd grieve more," she said. "I thought she'd be sad." She reached into the box of staples Garrett had brought and pulled out the homemade bread, then grabbed the sandwich fixings Hondo had provided out of the small refrigerator.

"She will be. She'll have a moment when she falls, but right now, something isn't letting her process what happened."

Laurel spread mustard over a piece of bread, then bent over the sink, clutching the porcelain. Her shoulders sagged. For a moment or two she fought the emotion. Everything inside Garrett made him want to hold her, comfort her, but he also knew sometimes grief needed space.

When her shoulders quivered, then shook, Garrett couldn't stay away. He crossed the small kitchen in two steps and placed his hands on her shoulders. He bent to her ear. "It's okay," he whispered.

Molly entertained herself across the room. He turned Laurel in his arms. Tears streamed down her face. She buried her head against his shoulder to hide them.

"I miss Ivy. I miss my family." Her voice had thickened with grief. Garrett rubbed her back, holding her close.

After he'd woken from the coma, alone in a hospital, with a new name, he hadn't had time to cry. God, he'd wanted to, but there was no one left to comfort him or hold him. His family was gone.

He could hold Laurel, though. His arms wrapped tighter around her. He kept his gaze locked on Molly, who'd found an afghan and a small cardboard box and was creating a fort under a beat-up end table.

"Can she see me?" Laurel whispered, her voice thick with tears.

"She's playing," Garrett said.

Laurel trembled against him. Then a calmness flowed through her. She stood in his arms, soft, welcoming.

Comfort shifted to something more, something else.

Something simmering beneath the surface. She cleared her throat and straightened, swiping at her wet cheeks. Through her lowered lashes, she looked up at him. "I'm okay now."

He stroked a tear from her cheek. "You don't have to be."

She glanced over at Molly. "Yeah, I do." Laurel pasted a smile on her face and strode over to Molly, hunkering down. "Whatcha doin', Molly Magoo? Can I come in your fort?"

Garrett turned back to the half-made picnic lunch, thankful Laurel had crossed the room. She and Molly had reawakened his emotions, emotions he couldn't afford to have.

He'd gone against his best instincts when he'd fallen in love with Lisa seven years ago. James had warned him, had told him that there would be secrets he could never tell his wife, lies he'd be forced to live. He'd even said there was a remote chance of danger from the enemy.

The enemy wasn't who'd gotten him... He'd been framed by one of his own. Of that he was certain.

He snagged some bottled water and a juice box from the refrigerator, completing their lunch. "Ready, ladies?" he called out.

Molly scooted from under the blanket and ran across the room. She peered into the makeshift picnic basket Garrett had created using a box. "Cookies?" She blinked up at him, those baby blues innocent and hopeful.

"What's a picnic without Hondo's cookies?" Garrett said. "Can you take this?" he asked Laurel. She grasped the box and he strode into his room. He unlocked the closet and entered a combination into a hidden safe. Quickly, he pulled out his dad's Remington.

He walked over to her. She tugged the box closer. "I'll take this. I like your hands free. In case the big kitty shows up again."

They walked out of the ranch house. The midday sun shone through a bright blue sky. Laurel gazed up. "I've never seen a color like that before."

"Welcome to the desert," Garrett said. "A little different from the East Coast, huh?"

"Considering they started today getting doused in snow, I'd say yes."

Molly bent over and picked up a pinecone. "Ooh. Sticky," she said, dropping it. She skipped around Garrett and Laurel, then ran a bit ahead.

"Molly," Garrett said with a warning tone.

She stopped and turned. "Sorry." She bowed her head and kicked a small rock.

"Just let me go first when we come to a thicket of trees," he said.

"What's a thicket?"

"A big group. Like right here."

Garrett stepped into a small grove. He bent down. "See where the winter grass is bent over? An animal slept here sometime last night or this morning."

He looked around and knelt beside a few tracks, two teardrops side by side. "Deer, probably mule deer in these parts."

Molly crouched beside him. "You can tell that?"

"Everything and everyone makes its mark." He shot her a sidelong glance. "Most everything can be traced or tracked. No one is invisible."

"My job was to analyze data from sources no one can imagine," Laurel said. "I know it's difficult to hide. But not impossible."

"Fair." Garrett stood. "But if it were easy to hide, Ivy would never have found me at all."

The admission didn't come easy, but Laurel needed to understand how difficult her life was about to become.

"There's a small pool nearby. We've had some rain this year, so it might be full."

They climbed over some more craggy rocks to a granite outcropping. The sun had warmed the rock, and below, a large pool of water glistened in the light.

"Just the place for our picnic."

He looked at the surroundings. Safe, and it was clear enough that he had a view where he could see anyone coming.

"Not exactly rolling hills," Laurel said, sitting down with the small box holding their lunch.

"I want to sit by here," Molly said, pointing at a small, flat rock.

"Just your size," Garrett said.

"Nothing rolling or quaint about West Texas," Garrett offered, pulling the sandwiches from the bag.

"It's dramatic," she admitted. "You can see forever."

"I like this spot. I come here sometimes. To think. Nothing small about this land. About seventy-six miles that way is the border with Mexico. North fifty miles and you're in New Mexico. On a clear day like today, you can see one hundred and fifty miles. Can't do that on the coast." He handed Molly a juice box.

"You miss D.C.?"

Garrett bit into his sandwich, swallowing past the lump in his throat, and considered his answer. "I miss the life I had." He missed his family. Every day. He no longer wanted to die along with them. The need for revenge made a body fight. Just to make the guilty pay.

Laurel's gaze fell to Molly. "I understand that. Going back will never be the same, will it?"

"Nothing is ever the same."

Molly crossed her legs and gazed into the water. "Can I touch it?"

"It's cold," Garrett warned.

Molly tiptoed to the edge of the pool, squatted in front of it and dipped her hand into the water. She snatched it back with a yelp.

"I'm not swimming in there." She raced back to Laurel and hugged her legs. "Too cold."

"Molly, do you see this rock?" Garrett picked up a piece of dark granite.

"It sparkles."

Molly's eyes widened as the stone glittered in the sunlight. "Can I keep it to show my mommy when she comes back?"

"You can have it," Garrett said, then lifted a familiar bag from the box.

Molly grinned. "Cookies?"

He set the treat aside. "Of course."

Molly popped a cookie in her mouth. When she finished it off, her leg swung on the side of the rock. "Can I go 'sploring?"

Laurel started to shake her head, but Garrett interrupted, "We've made too much noise not to drive the animals away." He turned to Molly. "Stay in sight. If you leave the clearing, we'll have to go back to the house."

"Cross my heart, hope to die, stick a nail in my eye," Molly said, making a motion across her chest.

A chuckle escaped Garrett. She was so like his Ella.

But so different, too. Molly jumped from the rock. She scampered to the edge of the clearing.

He folded Laurel's hand in his. "She'll be okay. I promise we're making too much noise for the cougar to be interested," he said.

"Bears?"

"Not here. Not enough vegetation and large animals."

Laurel dropped her half-eaten sandwich in the box and stood. She watched Molly. "I'm scared for her."

Garrett rose from the rock. "She's a strong girl. She's got a great aunt. You'll both make it through this."

"What if whoever killed Ivy gets away with it?"

Garrett couldn't stop his teeth from grinding together. No way would he let that happen. Not while he still lived. But he couldn't promise anything. The people after him had no morals, no conscience. If anyone got in their way, they killed them. And they didn't care about the innocent ones who got hurt in the process.

He turned Laurel in his arms and stared into her eyes. "However this goes, I'll make sure you and Molly find a way to be safe."

Laurel lowered her lids. "They might get away with it."

Garrett couldn't deny the truth of her words. Instead, he tilted her chin up with his finger. His heart stuttered at her pain-filled gaze. She'd lost her sister, her brother-in-law, one niece and nephew, and she might have lost her father. She'd lost the life she once had. He wanted to make everything go away, but he might not be able to. "I won't stop until I find them, Laurel."

She shivered in his arms. He tugged her a bit closer, his gaze falling on Molly. The little girl had hunkered down, stacking pinecones. He wrapped Laurel in his arms, pulling her close, and rested his cheek against her hair. Her warmth seeped into his skin, even as the sun shone down on his face.

For one moment he could comfort her. She sighed, leaning against him. "I wish we could stay here forever and the rest of the world would stop," she said.

Garrett closed his eyes, breathing in the fragrance of her hair. He turned and kissed her temple. Her arms tightened around his body. The comfort shifted into something more. Laurel tilted her head, her gaze stopping at his mouth. Garrett stilled, unable to stop the desire flaring just beneath the surface.

"I found a track, Sheriff Garrett," Molly shouted.

Laurel stiffened in his arms. He sighed and touched his finger to her lips. "Sometime soon," he promised. "When we can't be interrupted."

A pang of conscience needled the back of his neck. They were in danger and no one knew what was going to happen, but he couldn't deny the pull between him and Laurel. He'd been so alone for so long. Having her in his arms made him...made him feel hope again.

She squeezed his hand, her gaze warm, her cobalt eyes flaring with a hidden fire. With a sigh of regret, he walked across the small clearing where Molly hunkered down just at the edge.

"What have you found, sugar?"

She pointed a few feet past the row of pines. Garrett stilled. The track was human.

He peered past the trees into a clearing. The remains of a campfire had been hastily shoved aside, but the ash and rocks used to surround the small flames couldn't be mistaken.

Garrett's hand hovered over his weapon. His voice soft and low, he reached out a hand. "Come on, Molly."

"But I found a track."

"And you did well, but we need to go." He scooped her into his arms and strode away from the edge of the trees, one hand still inches from his weapon.

"What'd I do?" Molly whispered. "I didn't do anything wrong."

Laurel met him and he handed over the little girl. "What's wrong?" Laurel pulled the girl to her. "Shh, Molly."

"Company," he said, his voice calm.

Her eyes widened and a line of tension drew her mouth.

Molly squirmed in her arms. "I'm scared."

"Go back the way we came," Garrett said. He tugged the Beretta from beneath his jacket. "You have your SIG?"

She nodded.

"Be ready."

She shuffled Molly in her arms.

"Fire in the air if you see anything or anyone and then head back toward the ranch. I'll catch you. Can you find it?"

She nodded, placing herself at the edge of the clearing, ready to bolt, her hand gripping the weapon.

Garrett pushed through the pines and studied the ground. There were at least two sets of shoes. He sifted the dirt. The fire's remains were cold. They hadn't been watching. The tension in his chest eased a bit.

He glanced over at Laurel. She stood alert, watching everything. She would protect Molly with her life. He didn't like leaving them alone, but he needed to discover who these two people were. He followed the trail. The ground told many truths. One person fell, then scrambled to his feet. Garrett hit some granite rock and the trail vanished, but he picked it back up again on the other side.

Kneeling down, he studied the prints. "Who are you?"

Then he caught sight of a small impression. A kid's sneaker.

Aah. Quietly, he topped a hill. Below, a man hurried his wife and son across the terrain. The guy looked at him, and Garrett knew he recognized the sheriff's uniform, even without the star.

His face erupted in terror, but he didn't pull a weapon. He shoved his wife and son behind him and stared up at Garrett.

Not a great place to cross the border. Especially with a family. Was a coyote nearby? Most of the men who made a living illegally bringing people across the border made Garrett's stomach turn. They charged thousands of dollars to cross into the United States, and if their "customers" were lucky, the coyote got them to civilization. The unlucky ones ended up dead of thirst in the desert.

Garrett scanned the horizon, searching for signs of a coyote, but he didn't see anyone.

With a quick nod to the man, he turned and hurried back toward the clearing. He had to get Laurel and Molly to safety.

They might end up much like that man and his family. Living under the radar.

Unless Garrett succeeded where he and James had failed for the past eighteen months.

Garrett shoved his Stetson on his head. Now, though,

he had to succeed for more than just revenge—he had to succeed to protect two innocent lives.

He wouldn't lose. He couldn't.

LAUREL CARRIED MOLLY back into the cabin. Her niece was way too quiet. The little girl toyed with the collar Ivy had placed around the neck of her lion.

Garrett followed her in. "I'm canvassing the area once more. Lock the door behind me. I'll knock three times when I get back. And keep the gun handy."

"Shoot if someone else tries to get in," Laurel said. "Got it."

"Not if it's me." Garrett shut the door, putting the box of food on the floor.

Molly wiggled from Laurel's arms. "I want to go into my fort," she muttered. "I want Mr. Hairy Houdini to come with me."

"Want me to play with you?"

The little girl whispered into her stuffed animal's ear and shook her head, disappearing beneath the afghan.

Laurel sighed and put away the groceries, keeping a close eye on Molly.

Within a few minutes, the little girl was rubbing her eyes and yawning. It had been a tough few days. Not to mention just getting over strep throat.

Massaging her temple, Laurel scanned the room. They couldn't stay here forever. The only way out was to find who was behind Ivy's murder. And her father's disappearance. And stop them.

Garrett knew more than he was revealing. She believed that, and she didn't know who he was, really. That uneasy feeling at the base of her neck increased the urgency. She needed to *do* something. To protect Molly and herself. Not just for the moment, but for the future.

Laurel checked once more on her niece, but the little girl had zonked out.

Careful not to make any noise, she opened Garrett's office door and walked inside. She propped the door open so she could hear Molly or anyone outside and turned the machines on.

She'd had an idea. Maybe, just maybe, it would work.

Growing up with her father's ability to discover what his daughters were doing, Laurel had become adept at hiding her tracks. She'd joined the computer club at school. Yeah, it had helped her get into college, but more important, it had taught her a few tricks. Tricks that came in handy at her job, and that might come in even handier now.

She risked a lot doing this without Garrett here, but she had to try. It was her last chance or they'd have to go with Garrett's plan.

She navigated to a portal leading into some of the intelligence organization's unclassified databases.

When the log-in came up, she tapped her finger on the keyboard.

If she entered her information, she was starting a ticking clock. Eventually they would know she'd entered the system; they'd know what she discovered.

Garrett still hadn't returned.

She took a deep breath. She had to take the chance.

Her finger trembled typing in the password.

She was in.

Glancing at the time on the computer screen, she quickly

navigated to the travel database. Relatively low priority. She entered her father's name.

Access denied.

Interesting. She backed out, this time searching for Ivy's name, then hers. Finally, with her own name, she received a different screen.

Clicking on a link pulled up her personal data.

Status: Missing, presumed dead.

"What the hell do you think you're doing?"

Chapter Six

Strickland cursed. "Waiting around in this godforsaken town is getting us nowhere." The December Texas sun heated up the SUV and sweat trickled down his neck. He wiped his arm on his forehead. "Garrett Galloway isn't coming back."

"Do you think he knows the boss has found him?" Krauss asked, rolling down the window enough to allow a small crack. A soft, cool breeze flowed in. "I sure wouldn't stick around."

"Could be he ran. Or maybe he's hiding the woman and the girl."

"We're screwed either way, you know." Krauss's tone held nothing but resignation. "The boss'll find out we lost him, and we'll be dead. We're expendable and you know it. We both know it."

Krauss was right. But there had to be a way out. Maybe that deputy… Derek Bradley, aka Garrett Galloway, had lived in this town awhile. Strickland had discovered the people liked him. The waitress at the diner, the deputy, the local motel owner—they all thought the guy walked on water. Though that motel guy had shown Strickland the door too fast when his loopy sister had shown up and started yammering.

Maybe the tattooed freak knew more than he let on.

Strickland drummed his fingers on the steering wheel. "So, Krauss. You think Galloway would come back if real trouble visited Trouble, Texas?"

Krauss slowly nodded his head, a glimmer of hope reaching his eyes. "After what we know about both his identities, yeah. He's just enough of a hero to take the risk…if the bait is right."

"And I think I know exactly who—" Strickland's phone sounded. One glance at the number appearing on the screen and he could feel the blood drain from his face.

"It's the boss, isn't it?" Krauss said, a string of curses escaping from him. "What are you going to say?"

"I don't know." Strickland rubbed the back of his neck and tapped the phone. "Strickland."

"Imagine my surprise when I discovered your current location. Why didn't you tell me you were already in Trouble, Texas?"

At the biting tone of his boss's voice, he shivered, then gulped. He didn't have a good answer.

"Don't bother lying. There aren't a thousand people in that town. You come clean, Strickland, I might let you live…minus a body part or two."

Strickland met Krauss's gaze. The man's expression looked as if he'd scarfed down a large helping of bad fish. He'd seen the boss's handiwork. Missing fingers, missing toes, missing eyes…and worse.

"I—I saw a note Ivy Deerfield wrote when we went to set up the bomb." Strickland couldn't prevent the squeak in his voice as he lied. "She wrote down this sheriff's name. I just wanted to make sure she hadn't given anything—"

"How did you discover the connection between the McCallisters and Galloway?" his boss asked sharply.

"I didn't know about a link. I just had a bad feeling." More truth in those words. Strickland swallowed again. "You ordered us to follow up on loose ends. And to get rid of them."

"Which you enjoy a little too much," his boss muttered. "Okay, Strickland, I'll let you fix your little problem, but if I find out you're keeping something from me—"

"I've worked for you too long, boss," he said. Yeah, long enough to know that if he told her the truth of how he'd had them and lost them, she wouldn't just take a body part—she'd make him suffer and want to die.

Krauss just shook his head.

"Perhaps." The boss paused for a moment. "Well, Strickland, this may be your lucky day. I have Garrett Galloway's location for you. A gift from…a good friend."

The boss gave him a frequency. Krauss entered the number into the small tracking device. A red dot appeared on the screen. "He's in the mountains not far from here," Krauss said. "Rough country."

"Are you sure it's him? Or could this be his laptop or something?" Strickland asked.

A chuckle filtered through the phone. "It's inside him. You track that frequency, you'll have your target."

Strickland scratched at a surgical scar from a rotator-cuff repair a year or so ago. "That's not possible."

"Really? You have an inside track on the latest research and development of the agency, do you?"

Strickland gulped at the disdain in his boss's voice. "Of course not."

"You better be glad the chip isn't widely available. If I'd had one inserted inside you, I have a very good feeling you'd already be paying the price for some extracurricular activities."

The muscles in Strickland's back tensed. The only way out of this mess was clean it up and beg...or find out something he could bargain with.

"Find him, Strickland. And kill him. No mistakes." The phone call ended.

He grabbed the map from Krauss's hand and smiled for the first time since he'd realized the McCallister woman had escaped the bomb. "We have a pointer to Galloway. Which means we have McCallister and the kid, too. They're out in the middle of nowhere."

"Easy to dispose of bodies out there. No one will ever find them."

"Yeah." Strickland stared down at his phone. Now if he could only find a way that he wouldn't disappear either.

AT GARRETT'S BITING WORDS, Laurel's hands froze above the computer keyboard. She winced and whirled her chair around. If she'd thought he might be glad she'd taken the initiative to use her skills, that notion vanished the moment she took in his tight jaw and narrowed gaze.

"I had an idea," she protested. The niggling doubts that had skittered up her spine when she turned on the machine gnawed through her nerves. But what choice did they have?

"You've started the ticking clock." His cheek muscles pulsed.

That she had an answer for. "The clock would have

started anyway. We both know that. I just happened to control the start."

"Explain."

"I set up the signal to bounce all over the world. We're on a ticking clock—like you wanted, but thirty-six hours from now. Maybe forty-eight."

"How certain are you?"

"I wouldn't play with Molly's life like that. Or yours."

He studied her expression, then finally nodded his head. "Then sit down in the damn chair and get us some information. You started this. Let's see what your stint at the CIA can do for us."

Garrett snagged a kitchen chair from the other room and flipped it around, sitting astride the hard wood. She let out a long, slow breath. She knew her business, but her nerves crackled at his constant stare. Leaning forward, she focused on the monitor.

Soon she lost herself in the task, following path after path. She didn't know how long she'd been beating her head up against dead ends when a folder suddenly appeared.

Laurel stilled. "Look. The directory belongs to Ivy, but it's not official."

Garrett straightened in his chair. "Unauthorized?"

She nodded and clicked on the folder. It contained only one file. "It could be a trap."

"You've been at this awhile. What's your gut say?"

"To open it."

"Then do it."

She held her breath and double-clicked the file.

A password box came up.

"You know it?" Garrett asked.

"Maybe," Laurel said. She typed in her sister's anniversary.

Access denied.

Her children's names.

Access denied.

Her birthday.

Access denied.

"One more shot and I'm locked out. I'll have to start over," Laurel said, rubbing her eyes. "I may not even get access to the file again."

A long, slow breath escaped from Garrett. "You know your sister. Most of these passwords require at least one capital letter, one symbol and one number. And once you encrypt a file, if you forget the password, you're screwed. She'd have to be able to remember it."

Laurel drummed her fingers on the desk and sat back in the chair. She closed her eyes. "Ivy, what did you do?"

The room grew quiet, just the fan of the equipment breaking the silence.

Garrett didn't chatter, didn't interrupt her thoughts. She liked that about him. So many people didn't know when to simply be quiet.

"I may have it." She turned her head, meeting his gaze. "Ivy was older than me. She'd just started to date when Mom died. They had this special code. Even while Mom was in the hospital, she made Ivy promise to let her know if she was okay at nine o'clock. If there was trouble, there was a special message she'd leave on the pager."

"What was the code?"

"Mom's name, then nine-one-one, then an exclamation point. But if I'm wrong…"

"What do your instincts say?"

"That Ivy knew she was in danger and that she would pick something I knew." Laurel kneaded the back of her neck, her eyes burning. "She knew there was trouble."

"Do it."

Laurel swerved around and placed her hands on the keyboard. She couldn't make her fingers type in the password. What if she was wrong?

"Trust your gut." Garrett placed his hand on her shoulder. "Do it."

Laurel picked the keys out one at a time, taking extra care. Finally, she bit down on her lip and hit the enter key.

The machine whirred. The screen went blank.

"Please, no." She half expected a message with red flashing lights and alarms to appear stating the file had been destroyed.

A few clicks sounded and the word-processing program sprang to life.

Ivy's file opened. Laurel blinked. Then blinked again.

At the top of the file in bold letters were just a few words.

Derek Bradley is alive.
Alias: Sheriff Garrett Galloway.

THE WORDS SCREAMED from the page. Garrett groaned and gripped the wooden slats of the chair until his fingers cramped. Ivy had found out about him. This couldn't be happening. If she knew…others knew as well.

James's plan had failed. And God knew who he could trust.

Laurel launched out of her chair and faced him. "*You* are Derek Bradley? The traitor?" She backed away, shaking her head.

"Laurel—"

"You caused the deaths of dozens of agents. My father told me. He said you finally got paid back. You died with your wife…and daughter." Her hand slapped against her mouth, and her eyes widened. "It was a car bomb."

"I should have died. My wife and daughter *did* die," Garrett said, his voice holding a bitterness that burned his throat. How many times had he begged to die only to have first James, then the doctors, fight to save him? How many weeks had he lain in his hospital bed planning revenge when he discovered who had taken them from him?

Laurel's eyes were wide with horror. "Like Ivy."

Garrett gave a stiff nod. "I was running late on my way home from the office. I'd promised my wife I'd get home early, but I'd been hell-bent on tracking down an insider. I'd discovered a few hints, nothing concrete, but enough to keep me asking questions, pursuing leads in areas where I had limited need to know." He could barely look at the knowledge in her eyes. She knew what was coming, but he had to get it out. She had to understand. "I was running late, tying my tie. Lisa took my daughter and put her in the c-car." He cleared his throat. "I'd just walked out the door, dropped my keys. Lisa was tired of waiting. She turned on the engine and it blew. I had my back to the car or else the explosion would have taken me out."

"But why doesn't everyone know you're alive?"

Garrett shoved his hands back through his hair. "Your father. I don't know how, but he knew something was wrong at the agency. He'd seen some questionable information cross his desk. I was being framed. He came by right after the bomb went off. Just lucky, I guess, because he fixed it." Garrett raised his chin and met Laurel's gaze. "Derek Bradley died that night with his family."

Laurel's entire body shook. "My father called you a traitor."

"Your father didn't know if I would survive. He knew I wouldn't if whoever set the bomb realized their mistake. So he created a new identity and took me to a hospital in Texas, and I recuperated there. By the time I came out of the coma, I was dead and buried, and Garrett Galloway was born."

"How could no one find out?"

"I was in a coma for months, under another name. James tried to identify the leak, but there were no leads. By the time I woke up the case was closed. I had several months of physical therapy."

"If you're telling the truth, why didn't he warn Ivy?" Laurel's pleading gaze tugged at Garrett. She paced back and forth, her movements jerky, uncoordinated. She swiped at her eyes. "Why didn't my father protect Ivy? He could have told her to quit. She might still be alive."

"I don't know." Garrett stepped in front of her and took her shoulders, tilting his head to force her to look him in the eyes. "I know your father. James McCallister loved his family more than anything. If you want to blame anyone, blame me. I shouldn't have stayed Garrett

Galloway this long. I let your father convince me he was closing in on the traitor, that if they thought I was still dead they'd eventually get complacent. I agreed to let him continue the search."

"Dad could convince someone in North Dakota to buy ice in the winter," Laurel said, shaking her head. "He always thought he knew the best for everyone else."

"He believed I'd take too many risks. He was right." Garrett had to face the truth. "I'm sorry, Laurel. So sorry. If I'd come back, maybe I could have forced the traitor's hand."

She scrubbed her hands over her face and stepped out of his embrace. "This doesn't make sense. Ivy knew about you and your case. She said you were right. You have to know *something*."

"I discovered there was a mole in the organization, but I never figured out who."

"Maybe Ivy did." Laurel's expression turned eager. She plopped into the computer chair and scrolled down her sister's file. Garrett leaned over her shoulder. She'd taken his identity in stride. The more time he spent with James's daughter, the more Garrett recognized the similarities. Smart, tenacious, optimistic. Traits he admired in his mentor. Qualities he liked in Laurel. A little too much.

He shifted closer, aware of the pulse throbbing at her throat, the slight increase in her breathing. He wanted to squeeze her shoulder, offer her encouragement, but he didn't want to distract her either. He backed away, forcing himself to focus on the file. Lists of operations, lots of questions, brainstorming. Ivy had been smart, curious and methodical. And her quest had gotten her killed.

As Laurel scrolled, an uneasy tingle settled at the

2 FREE BOOKS

ABSOLUTELY FREE · GUARANTEED

We'd like to send you another 2 excellent reads from the series you're enjoying now **ABSOLUTELY FREE** to say thank you for choosing to read one of our fine books, and to give you a real taste of just how much fun the Harlequin™ reader service really is. There's no catch, and you're under no obligation to buy anything — EVER! Claim your 2 FREE Books today.

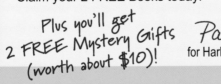

Plus you'll get 2 FREE Mystery Gifts (worth about $10)!

Pam Powers
for Harlequin Reader Service

VALUE:	COMBINED BOOK COVER PRICE:	POSTAGE DUE:
	Over $10 (US)/Over $10 (CAN)	$0

COMPLETE YOUR POSTCARD AND RETURN IT TODAY

Plus 2 FREE Mystery Gifts!

2 FREE BOOKS

ABSOLUTELY FREE • GUARANTEED

CLAIM YOUR FREE GIFTS

YES! Please send me my **2 FREE BOOKS** and **2 FREE GIFTS.** I understand that, as explained on the back of this card, I am under no obligation to purchase anything!

2 FREE Books

M-8801-0792-MG

Affix sticker here

❏ I prefer the regular-print edition
182/382 HDL GF6X

❏ I prefer the larger-print edition
199/399 HDL GF6X

FIRST NAME	LAST NAME

ADDRESS

APT.#	CITY

STATE/PROV.   ZIP/POSTAL CODE

HARLEQUIN™ READER SERVICE —Here's How It Works:

Accepting your 2 free Harlequin Intrigue® books and 2 free gifts (gifts valued at approximately $10.00) places you under no obligation to buy anything. You may keep the books and gifts and return the shipping statement marked "cancel." If you do not cancel, about a month later we'll send you 6 additional books and bill you just $4.74 each for the regular-print edition or $5.49 each for the larger-print edition in the U.S. or $5.24 each for the regular-print edition or $5.99 each for the larger-print edition in Canada. That is a savings of at least 13% off the cover price. It's quite a bargain! Shipping and handling is just 50¢ per book in the U.S. and 75¢ per book in Canada.* You may cancel at any time, but if you choose to continue, every month we'll send you 6 more books, which you may either purchase at the discount price or return to us and cancel your subscription. *Terms and prices subject to change without notice. Prices do not include applicable taxes. Sales tax applicable in N.Y. Canadian residents will be charged applicable taxes. Offer not valid in Quebec. Books received may not be as shown. All orders subject to credit approval. Credit or debit balances in a customer's account(s) may be offset by any other outstanding balance owed by or to the customer. Please allow 4 to 6 weeks for delivery. Offer available while quantities last.

BUSINESS REPLY MAIL
FIRST-CLASS MAIL   PERMIT NO. 717   BUFFALO, NY

POSTAGE WILL BE PAID BY ADDRESSEE

HARLEQUIN READER SERVICE
PO BOX 1867
BUFFALO NY 14240-9952

NO POSTAGE
NECESSARY
IF MAILED
IN THE
UNITED STATES

If offer card is missing write to: Harlequin Reader Service, P.O. Box 1867, Buffalo NY 14240-1867 or visit www.ReaderService.com

nape of Garrett's neck. Every operation involved James somehow. Several involved Garrett; some didn't.

"Slow down," he said softly, his voice tense.

"Ivy had more questions than answers." Laurel shot him a sidelong glance then stilled her hand. "What's wrong?"

That she read him meant he was out of practice. He guarded his expression. "Probably nothing."

"I can see it in your eyes." She snapped the words in challenge. "You've already lied about your identity, Derek. Don't lie about anything else. I deserve the truth. So does Ivy. And Molly."

"I'm Garrett now." He stiffened, but knew she was right. If something happened to him, she couldn't be in the dark. She had to be cautious. Around everyone. "James was involved in all the cases Ivy investigated."

Laurel's back straightened and her expression hardened. "My father is not a traitor. Who else was involved?"

"I didn't say he was—"

"You were thinking it. Tell me."

He couldn't deny the thought had crossed his mind.

"I was involved," he said.

"You know, Garrett, sometimes you have to have faith in the people you love. Even when the whole world seems screwed up, there are people who live by honor out there." She looked over her shoulder at him. "You're proof of that. My father trusted you with his family when he was in trouble. So have I. My father deserves the same consideration. Unless you really are a traitor."

Man, Laurel McCallister went right for the jugular with a few well-placed words.

"Then why aren't you afraid of me? Are you afraid that I might betray you?"

"You would have killed us already. Instead, you saved us. You sacrificed your hideaway. You put yourself at risk. Face it, Garrett, you're a hero. Just like my dad believed." Laurel scrolled to the end of the file. "There's a link here."

She clicked it. Another password. She tried the same one.

Access denied.

After three more attempts, Laurel shoved back from the keyboard with a frustrated curse. "I'm out of ideas."

Laurel shook her head, and he could see the fatigue and disappointment on her face. He kneaded her shoulders. "You're good with that machine. Is there another way to figure out the password? Are you a code breaker?"

"It's not my area, but…" She drummed her fingers on the table. "Maybe I can do one better." She chewed on her lip. "I developed a code-breaking computer program with some friends when I was in college." She winced. "We nearly got kicked out of the computer-science department when our adviser found out. I could run it from here, but it will take a while."

"As in we'll be connected to the network for a long time?"

Laurel nodded, and then her eyes brightened. "Unless I download the file."

At this point, it was worth the risk. "Do it."

Laurel clicked through options so quickly Garrett's eyes nearly crossed. "You never hesitate."

"My dad and Ivy have the gift of thinking on their feet. I do better with zeros and ones."

"Mommy!" Molly screamed at the top of her lungs. "Daddy!"

The terrorized cries pierced the air. The sound speared Garrett's heart. He didn't hesitate, throwing open the door to the living room.

At the same time, Laurel exploded from her chair, racing to her niece.

Molly sat straight on the sofa, her cheeks red, sweat dripping down her face, her eyes screwed up tight.

Laurel sat beside Molly and wrapped the little girl in her arms. "Shh, Molly Magoo. I've got you."

Laurel rocked her back and forth, but Molly refused to open her eyes, shaking her head so hard her hair whipped around, sticking to her tearstained face. She clutched at Laurel.

"Is she still asleep?"

"She's clinging to you. She knows you're here."

Laurel hugged Molly closer. "What do I do? This has never happened before."

Molly's sobs gutted Garrett's heart. Ella hadn't had a lot of nightmares, but she'd watched part of *Jurassic Park* at a friend's house and that evening the night terrors had stalked her. Only one thing had calmed her.

Molly struggled against Laurel. "You took me away," she whimpered.

Laurel's face went pale. The agony in her expression made Garrett hurt for her. "Give her to me," he said.

Laurel hesitated.

"I know what to do," he whispered.

Reluctantly, she handed the twisting little girl to Garrett. He sat down in a large overstuffed chair and held

Molly close to his chest. "It's okay, sugar," he said, making his voice soft and deep and hypnotic. He snagged a blanket and wrapped her like a burrito inside it, one arm tight around her.

He rocked her slowly and started singing in an almost whisper. "The ants go marching one by one, hurrah, hurrah. The ants go marching one by one, hurrah, hurray. The ants go ma-ar-ching one by one, the last one stops to look at the sun, and they all go marching down, in the ground, to get out of the rain."

The melodic, low tone of the song echoed in the room. He rubbed her back in circles. Her sobs quieted a bit.

Garrett sang the second verse, all the while rocking her, rubbing her back, holding her close.

Molly's cries turned to hiccups and finally softened. His chest eased a bit. Just like Ella. He looked up. Laurel's face had turned soft and gentle, and awed.

She hitched her hip on the arm of the chair and fingered Molly's locks. The little girl's eyes blinked. She opened her baby blues, looking up at Garrett, then at Laurel.

"Mommy?" she asked. "Daddy?"

"They aren't here, sugar," Garrett said. "But your aunt Laurel is. She won't let anything happen to you. Neither will I."

Molly bit down on her lip. "There was a 'splosion. Daddy's car burned like in the fireplace."

A tear trickled down Laurel's face. "Yes, honey, it did."

"Are Mommy and Daddy coming back?" she asked, her voice small, fearful.

Laurel glanced at Garrett. He warred with what to do, what to say. He simply nodded. It was time.

He tightened his hold on Molly. Laurel cleared her throat. "Honey, they aren't coming back, but they're watching over you. They're in heaven."

Tears welled in Molly's eyes. "Even Matthew and Michaela?"

"Even them, sweetie." Laurel handed her Mr. Houdini. Molly hugged the lion close.

Tears rolled down her face. "I want them back."

Laurel sank closer to Garrett. He shifted and she nestled next to him. Her arm wrapped around Molly, her cheek resting on the little girl's head. "So do I, Molly Magoo. So do I."

Molly clutched her stuffed animal. She didn't scream, as if the pain was too much for that. She laid her head on Garrett's chest. Fat tears rolled down her cheeks.

"Sing to me," she pleaded. "My heart hurts."

"The ants go marching…" Garrett fought against the emotions closing his throat. Memories too horrible and too deep slammed into him. Nights lying in the hospital bed after he'd awakened, reaching out his hand for Lisa's or for Ella's and no one had been there.

Just anonymous nurse after nurse—or no one at all.

Laurel leaned against him, her shoulders silently shaking. He knew she was crying. She buried her face in his neck.

Garrett held on to them, the children's tune now a mere murmur. Soon Molly went still in his arms.

He fell silent.

Sunlight streamed into the window, but he could tell from the angle it was low in the sky. Late afternoon.

He looked over at Laurel. Her eyes were red. "It breaks my heart," she whispered.

His own emotions raw and on the surface, he gave

a quiet nod. "I should put her in bed. She'll wake up at some point, but she needs the rest."

Laurel shifted away from him and he rose, taking the precious bundle into his bedroom. He pulled off her shoes and tucked her under the covers. He kissed her forehead. "Sweet dreams, sugar."

His arms felt empty. His throat tightened as the past overtook him. His own little girl, afraid. His Ella hadn't known a nightmare would come. Neither had Molly.

He turned and Laurel stood in the doorway watching him, her face ravaged with grief. His own festered just beneath the surface. Part of him wanted to escape the claustrophobia of his bedroom, to run to the top of a mountain and shout his fury. Instead, he walked toward her and she backed up. He stepped into the living room and closed the door softly behind him. The latch clicked.

She said nothing, and he didn't know what to say. Molly's tears had torn away the defensive emotional wall he'd worked so diligently to build over the past eighteen months.

She simply walked into his arms, and he could do nothing but enfold her, cling to her and struggle to contain the dam of feelings that threatened to break free.

Laurel stood there silently for several minutes. Her warmth seeped through his shirt. How long since he'd just let himself be this close to someone?

Much too long.

"Thank you," she said. She eased back and touched his cheek with her hand, her whispering caress soft and tender.

"You handled her well. She'll cry more. It won't be over today, but she'll make it. So will you."

He kissed her forehead and she wrapped her arms

around his waist, hugging him tight. He knew she just needed someone to cling to, but he couldn't ignore the slight pickup of his heartbeat. She was too vulnerable. And so was he. Laurel and Molly's presence reminded him of a pain he'd barely endured. Now somehow he had to find the strength to help them survive.

A small whimpering filtered from his bedroom.

"Go to her." Garrett stepped away. "She needs family."

Laurel gripped his hand and kissed his cheek. "You're a good man, Garrett Galloway." She disappeared behind the door and he heard her softly speaking to Molly.

Once he was certain the little girl was calm, he grabbed his Beretta from atop the refrigerator, where he'd stashed it, and strode onto the porch. The sun had turned red as it set on the western side of the ranch. The face of the mountain had turned light red and purple. Garrett sucked in a deep breath of mountain air. He exhaled, shuddering, and gripped the wooden rail until his knuckles whitened.

He blinked quickly, shoving back the overwhelming emotions that threatened to escape.

Molly and Laurel could rip what was left of his heart to shreds. When he'd come to and realized Lisa and Ella had paid the ultimate price for his job, only the need for revenge had kept him alive those first few months during therapy. He'd buried the grief deep in a hole where his heart had once resided.

Garrett scrubbed his face with his hands. Molly had reminded him of what it was like to protect someone who was truly innocent. And Laurel. God, that woman made him want what he couldn't have. He couldn't even let himself think about her that way. Not until whoever had killed his family—and hers—was no longer a threat.

A rustle in the trees made Garrett still. He focused on the movement. For several seconds he watched. Another slight shift of the pine needles, a scrape. Not the wind.

Someone, or something, was out there.

He gripped his weapon and moved behind the stone pillar at the corner of the house. If a weapon had a bead on him, he needed cover.

Once he decided to move, he'd have only a split second.

A shadow shifted in the fading sunlight. Two eyes peered at him from between the pines.

Garrett stepped off the porch. "So, you're back."

Chapter Seven

Laurel snuggled Molly next to her. The little girl twisted the flannel of her Christmas nightgown. It had been a present from Ivy when she'd realized Molly wouldn't be able to attend the pageant that fateful night.

When Laurel had followed Molly into the cabin's bedroom, her niece had pulled her mother's gift from the duffel and silently handed it to Laurel.

"You can wear my T-shirt, Molly Magoo," Laurel had said, barely able to speak.

"Mommy said Santa would know where to find me if I wore my special nightgown. He'd know I was being a good girl even if I couldn't be an angel." Molly had looked up at her. "Santa can find me here, can't he?"

"Of course he can. He knows you've been a very good girl this year."

Laurel stroked Molly's hair. "I'll have to find Christmas for you, Molly," she said under her breath. "Somehow."

The little girl hugged her lion close, her face buried in its mane. Her breathing slowed, growing even. She sighed and tucked her tiny hand under her cheek. Laurel held her breath, but Molly simply snuggled down under the covers.

Hopefully sleep would bring peace. For a while.

Minutes ticked by. Laurel's heart ached with an emptiness she'd never imagined. She wanted Ivy to walk through the door, tell her it was all a mistake. Tell her this had all been a bad dream, a setup. One of their father's elaborate plans.

A small part of her still hoped that were true, but she knew it wasn't. She'd heard her father's voice on the phone. This had nothing to do with the intelligence game he played. Every moment was real.

Her father was probably dead as well.

She and Molly were alone.

Laurel dug her fingernails into her palm, savoring the bite of pain. She wasn't dreaming—even though she was in the midst of her own nightmare.

Her niece's blond hair fell over her forehead. At least Laurel had Molly. The little girl gave Laurel a reason to not curl up in a ball and disappear. She'd never imagined her heart could feel so empty. That loneliness could suffocate her as if she were drowning.

Garrett had lost his wife and daughter. Laurel couldn't imagine the agony he'd gone through. How had he survived? Alone, with his entire past erased, how had this not destroyed him?

Laurel glanced at the door. She could stay in this room for the evening. Every muscle in her body ached with exhaustion and fatigue. Each time she blinked, grit scraped her eyes, but for the first time in days, she felt safe. At least for the next twenty-four hours.

She should sleep, but Garrett was out there. Alone.

Her father had told her Derek Bradley was a traitor, but the more she recalled the conversations, the more she recognized the inconsistencies. Her father was an excellent liar, no doubt, but he'd been cagey about Bradley. He'd set up the doubts, so she would be able to trust him.

"Derek took too many risks," James McCallister had said last Thanksgiving. *"He paid the price. So did his family. Traitors always get what's coming to them. Eventually."*

Her father had never called Derek Bradley a traitor.

Something from around Laurel's heart eased, and she realized that somewhere deep inside she'd still had doubts. They were gone now. Besides, her image of a man who would sell out his country for money didn't mesh with the man who could sing Molly into calmness from hysteria.

As she'd said to Garrett, at some point you had to let faith lead you. Careful not to jostle Molly, Laurel rose from the bed and padded across the room. The little girl didn't stir. Laurel pressed her hand against the door and slowly turned the knob. She opened it and eased out of the bedroom.

The living room was empty.

She peeked into his workroom, but he wasn't there. The encryption program still ran.

Finally she looked out the front window. He stood on the porch, his back to her, staring out at the sunset. His entire body screamed tension. As if he wanted to be left alone.

Laurel hesitated. She could return to the bedroom for the night, plant herself in front of the computer and wait, hoping the program would find the password, or she could go to Garrett. Except she knew what would happen the moment she touched him. They were both vulnerable. They both needed something only the other could provide.

She opened the front door. The cold gust of wind made her shiver. The last rays of light disappeared behind a mountain and deep purplish-blue painted the sky, rimmed at the horizon with a splash of pink and red. "Garrett?"

He didn't turn around. She glanced down. He held his gun at the ready. She froze.

"In the trees," he said softly.

She followed his gaze. Two piercing blue eyes peered at them, intent and calm.

The cougar.

"He's back," Laurel whispered.

"Cats are curious, but cautious. He won't come closer."

Garrett walked down the steps and picked up a large stone, tossing it toward the animal. The cat scampered off into the trees. "We need to keep Molly inside," he said. "That cat's learned people are a source of food. Probably eating after some of the border crossers left provisions behind."

He shoved his gun into the back of his jeans and escorted her inside the house. "How's Molly?"

"I'd guess out for the night, though she'll probably be up before dawn."

"Which reminds me." Garrett flicked the dead bolt in place, then shoved a chair underneath the doorknob before activating the sensors.

"You think that will stop her?"

"She'll make a lot of noise trying to get that chair out. I'll hear the little Houdini."

Laurel couldn't help but smile. "She's just like Ivy. When we were kids—"

"I would imagine she got you into a lot of trouble."

"Dad would get so furious at us. I tried to take the fall

a time or two, but Ivy wouldn't let me. She was so much fun. I would have never had all those adventures if not for her." Laurel sighed. "I'll always miss her, won't I?"

Garrett double-checked the chair then faced her, his expression solemn. "I won't tell you it gets better. The scab may get a little tougher."

She chanced a glance at him under her lashes. His stance was a bit awkward, as if he didn't know what to say either. Maybe she'd been wrong. She should have just turned in with Molly.

"We'd better check on the computer—" he started.

"I guess I'll turn in—" she said at the same time.

She shifted from one foot to the other. "I just looked at the program's status," Laurel said. "Still running. No answers."

"I see. Then I guess it's good-night."

Something solemn and painful had settled behind his eyes. And vulnerable. She didn't want to leave him. She didn't want to be alone tonight. She crossed to him, her heart rate escalating with each step. She knew exactly what she was inviting. So did he.

She stopped inches away from him, still staring into his eyes. They darkened into a deep mahogany flaring with want, maybe with need.

"What are you doing, Laurel?" His voice had grown deep, husky.

Her touch tentative, she placed her hand on his chest. She needed him. "We're safe for a while," she said. "Aren't we?"

"That's debatable," he said softly.

He covered the hand resting on his chest with his and lifted her palm to his lips. He nipped at the pad then threaded his fingers through hers. "You know this is a mistake," he said, his voice barely audible. "You don't know me. Not really."

A shiver skated down her spine at his words, but the naked longing in his eyes shoved aside her doubts.

She knew him.

"I've watched you. You gave up your safe existence to help me and Molly. You calmed her fears tonight. I know everything I need to know."

"Even though the world thinks I'm a traitor."

"I know the truth." She shook her head, leaning closer, wanting more than anything for him to stop talking and kiss her.

"What if you're wrong, Laurel?" He cupped her cheek and held her gaze captive. Her heart fluttered in response. His thumb grazed her cheek. "What if I'm a man who would do anything to get what he wants? I'm good at keeping secrets. And I'm *very* good at telling lies."

She couldn't stop staring at his lips. "I can tell when you're lying, Garrett. Your eyes grow dark, and the right corner of your mouth tightens just a bit."

Would his mouth be hard or soft, passionate or gentle against hers when they kissed?

"I don't want you," he said softly, his breath whispering against her cheek as he moved closer to her lips.

"You're bluffing."

"You're too trusting." He lowered his mouth to her ear. "But I don't have the strength to pull away."

She smiled. "Now you're telling the truth."

With a groan he fastened his lips to hers and wrapped his arms around her. She didn't hesitate. She clung to him and let his mouth drive away the memories of the past week. For this wonderful moment all she could think about was his touch, his mouth exploring hers, the taste of him.

He lifted his head. "Be very sure, because I won't let you go all night long."

She didn't answer, just pulled his mouth to hers once more. He groaned and swept her into his arms. With a long stride he carried her into the smaller bedroom, closing the door behind them. She didn't notice the Spartan furniture; her only focus was on Garrett. She used the name of the sheriff she'd come to know, not the name of the man he used to be.

"I don't know what the future holds, but I know what I want right now," Laurel said. "I need you, Garrett."

"Not more than I need you." Gently he laid her on the bed, following her down, covering her with his weight.

She didn't resist, but relished the feel of him on top of her. With a groan, he buried his lips against her neck, exploring the pulse points at the base of her throat. Laurel threaded her hands through his hair. Every kiss made her belly tingle with need. She wanted more.

"Please," she whispered. "Kiss me."

"I am," he said softly, nipping at the delicate skin just below her ear.

"Garrett." She couldn't stop the frustration from lacing her voice.

"How about here?" He nibbled the lobe of her ear. "Or here?" He worked his way down, shifting her shirt aside, and tasted the skin just above her collarbone.

Laurel stirred beneath him until finally he raised his head. He tugged at her lower lip. "Or how about here?"

His mouth swooped down and captured hers. He pressed her lips open and she moaned in relief that she could finally taste him. She returned his kiss for kiss.

Her hands seemed to have a mind of their own, exploring the strength of his back through his shirt. She hated the barrier between them. She wanted to touch him, skin to skin. She wedged her hands between them, unbuttoning his shirt and shoving the material off his shoulders.

He stilled above her, looking at her, his gaze intense, hesitant, full of warning. Her fingertips paused when she encountered roughened skin.

Burns. The car bomb.

He let out a slow sigh then moved off of her, lying on his back. "I should have warned you." His shirt fell open and she pulled away. His chest was mostly unmarred, except for a long surgical scar down his midline.

"You think what happened changes anything? It makes me want you even more." She didn't hesitate, but straddled his hips and traced the scar.

He looked up at her and caught her fingertip. "My entire back was turned when the car exploded. There was a lot of damage. I had several rounds of skin grafts. During surgery my heart stopped. I died on the operating table and they cracked me open." His voice was detached, his jaw tight, holding back emotion. "It's not pretty," he said. "It will never be pretty."

"And if I could have Ivy back, you think the scars would make me love her less? You earned these badges of courage." Laurel moved her hands up to his shoulders, venturing a tentative touch on the puckered skin. "Does it hurt?"

"I can't always feel when you touch me. And in some places the nerve endings go a little haywire, but mostly no. It's healed as much as it's going to."

He didn't move, didn't try to pull her to him, didn't try

to kiss her. He simply lay there gazing up at her. "You don't have to do this."

"Neither do you, but you're the bravest man I know and I don't think you'll chicken out now," she said and leaned forward, gently, tenderly pressing her lips to his. "I want this. Now. With you. Tell me if I hurt you."

She lifted her shirt over her head and removed her bra. His eyes hooded as he cupped her breast in his hand and drew his thumb across her nipple. It beaded in response and a sharp tingle lit in her belly. A small whimper escaped her and she gripped his shirt.

He smiled, the defensive expression in his eyes darkening to desire once again. "I can't believe you want me." Garrett tugged her down to him, his palm against the small of her back, rocking her hips against his, his desire evident.

"Can you feel me now?" she whispered, shifting her body, evoking a groan from him.

"Definitely." He flipped her over and threw his shirt off the side of the bed. "You're an amazing woman, Laurel McCallister."

She wrapped her arms around him, blinking back the hurt for him when she encountered the mottling of scars down his back and a few strips of unblemished skin. She yanked him down closer and wrapped her legs around his hips. "Show me how amazing you think I am. I don't want to wait another second."

THEY WERE IN the middle of nowhere. Still.

Strickland peered out the front window. The SUV's headlights broke through the early evening, but a cluster of trees and an avalanche of rocks blocked the path. They'd reached the end of the road.

"Damn it." He hit the steering wheel. "How far is Bradley from here?"

Krauss studied the screen. The red dot was immobile. "Couple of miles, according to this. He's not moving."

Strickland rubbed the stubble on his chin. "Give me the city any day of the week. I hate the West. Too much godforsaken territory to cover."

"We going back to Trouble?"

"Not a chance. Get your canteen," Strickland ordered. "We're going after him. He won't expect us to track him out here."

"We're really heading out at night?"

"You want to tell the boss we're taking the evening off?" Strickland asked.

Krauss muttered to himself as he grabbed the water and his weapon. "This is a mistake. Weren't you a Cub Scout or something? We don't know the country. Anything could be out there. It's easy to get turned around in the darkness."

Strickland tapped the glowing red light on Krauss's monitor. "We've got a beacon to light the way. Besides, we don't have a choice. Now come on."

They exited the SUV and Strickland grabbed an M16, slinging it over his shoulder. "I'll tell you one thing, though. I'm not hauling those bodies down this mountain. Once we kill them, we leave them to rot."

GARRETT COULDN'T BELIEVE Laurel was here, in his bed, beneath him, with her long, lean legs wrapped around him. His body surged in response to her arch.

She grasped his shoulders and her hands moved to his back.

He couldn't believe she hadn't politely said good-night and walked away. Garrett didn't think about the scars on his back that often. Just when he'd rub against something the wrong way and the nerves fired, as if a thousand pins were stabbing him.

Laurel nipped at his ear. "I want you," she whispered. "Now."

No more than he wanted her.

He rubbed his chest against her, reveling in the feeling of their skin touching. With each caress of his chest against her budded nipples, she let out a low moan, shivering against him. He moved again, and this time, she hugged him close, tilting her pelvis into his hardness. God, she was so responsive. She didn't hold anything back. He'd never been with a woman who was so honest about what she wanted.

Her hands worked their way between them to the waist of his pants, tugging at his stubborn belt in frustration.

He lifted away, forcing her legs to release him. He hated she no longer held him captive, but he wanted her wild for him. He wanted to drive them both so crazy that the past and the past week would vanish...at least for a moment.

With a quick flick, he removed the leather belt and threw it to the side of the bed before unbuttoning the waist. She shoved at his hand, but he gripped her fingers. "Not yet."

He lifted her hands above her head, pinning them down with one of his own. He gazed at the rise and fall of her chest. Her breathing quickened beneath his gaze, her blue eyes transformed into cobalt pools. That she trusted him enough to give him control caused his body to throb in response. He let his fingers stroke her cheek and drew her lip down. Her tongue snaked out to taste his finger. He smiled at her and let her suckle for a moment before taking his hand around her jawline, down her throat, where the pulse raced.

Her legs shifted but he trapped her beneath him. With a butterfly-light touch he teased her breasts, circling one nipple, then the other. Her chest flushed; her back arched. He followed a trail, teasing her, relishing in the soft sounds of pleasure coming from her lips.

"Garrett," she finally pleaded. She didn't tug her hands away, though. She wanted more. And he wanted to give her more than she'd dreamed of.

Ever so slowly he explored each delectable inch of skin, first with his fingertips, then with his lips and finally with his tongue. When he reached her waist, tasting the sweetness just above her belly button, she sucked in her stomach. He flicked open the button of her jeans.

Prolonging her pleasure, and his painful desire, he slid down the zipper and eased her pants over her hips. Simple white bikini panties hid her from his gaze.

Garrett tugged at the elastic, swallowing. He throbbed against his zipper. He was going to lose control. He'd been determined to drive her mad, but he was losing his mind.

And his heart.

He rose to his knees and tugged at the elastic waist.

She wrenched her hands from his grip and sat up. "I can't take it anymore," she said. She shoved her jeans and the small scrap of cloth down her legs, leaving her bare to his view.

God, she was beautiful.

Without hesitation she pushed against his zipper. His body surged.

"I'm too close," he said, his voice tight.

"So am I," she countered. "Make love to me, Garrett."

He gritted against the sensitivity of his body as he shucked off the rest of his clothes. He reached into the bedside table and grabbed a condom.

Her legs parted for him and she pulled him to her. She didn't play coy or hesitate. "Make love to me, Garrett. Now."

Unable to resist, with one thrust, he sank deep inside her.

She was ready for him, welcoming, hot and needy. He lost himself in her. The past disappeared, the uncertainty.

She cocooned him in her warmth. With each stroke, she sighed, and then the rhythm built, slowly at first, then stronger, faster, more intense.

His heart raced; his body trembled. He wanted to feel her fall apart in his arms. She tightened around him and he couldn't hold off. He thrust against her and his body pulsed in release. He sagged on top of her, the rhythmic quivering of her body gripping him.

She'd fallen over the edge with him.

For a moment he couldn't move, letting his heart slow, feeling her heartbeat calm.

"Wow," she mumbled, stroking his hair.

He moved off of her, disposed of the condom and spooned her. She felt so good, so right lying against him. He kissed her temple, wrapping one leg around hers, unwilling to let her escape from his embrace.

"Yeah. *Wow* about covers it."

She wiggled her back end against him before settling down. She gripped one of his hands between hers.

"I feel like a boneless jellyfish," she said. "I never want to move from here."

He didn't either. He stared at the wall, just listening to her breathe. In and out, soft and steady. He hadn't planned this. But he couldn't find it inside him to regret.

That in itself made him wince. What had he done?

He toyed with a small curl of hair against her cheek. She was so soft and yet so strong. And so smart. Her fingers had flown across that keyboard and he had seen her analyzing the problem, creating a solution and acting on it.

More than that, she was brave. She hadn't hesitated to protect Molly.

"I can feel you thinking," she said softly. She turned in his arms and looked at him. "What about? Regrets?"

A hesitant expression had settled on her face. He kissed her nose. "No regrets, even though—"

"Don't," she pleaded. "I don't want to think about what's happening. Not yet. Can't we just be, with nothing between us? Just for a few minutes."

"Of course." He wrapped his leg over her hip, pulling her against him, saying nothing.

She played with the smattering of hair on his chest for a moment, then sighed. "But it won't go away. They're coming."

Her hands slowed then stilled. "Do you think Dad is okay?"

"Do you want lies or truth?"

"Truth."

He twirled a strand of her hair. "I don't know. I'd have hoped he'd get word to me by now. Somehow."

"You're worried."

"James has kept himself alive a long time."

"Are you trying to convince me or yourself?" Laurel asked, her voice laced with sadness.

"Both, maybe."

She huddled into him and he wrapped his arms around her. She went quiet for several minutes, and Garrett wondered if she'd fallen asleep. He hoped so. She could use the rest.

"How do we catch them, Garrett?" Her breath kissed his bare chest. "They haven't made a mistake."

The despair in her words touched his very soul. More because he couldn't guarantee anything. Not even her safety. All he knew was he'd do his damnedest to keep her and Molly alive.

His arms gripped her tighter. "Actually, they have made a mistake. Your sister was killed because she identified evidence. Which means—"

"They left a trail," Laurel finished.

"Once you find a way into that file, we could have the answer." Garrett closed his eyes and stroked her hair. An answer to the revenge that had eaten away at his gut since he'd woken up from that coma with his life changed forever.

Lisa and Ella might finally be able to rest in peace. Maybe he would, too. He moved away from Laurel. He unwrapped himself from her and sat on the side of the bed, his head in his hands.

Laurel sucked in a breath from behind him. He'd forgotten about his back. He grabbed for his shirt. "I'm sorry."

"Don't," she whispered.

The bed shifted and she moved behind him. She rubbed the base of his neck. He groaned, feeling the tension that had been sitting there for so long dissipate. Her hands drifted down, in and out of his ability to feel.

Her touch caressed his lower back. "Can you feel me?" she asked.

"Mmm-hmm."

She nipped at the back of his neck with her teeth. "How about now?"

"Oh, yes." He let his head fall forward while she explored.

Her touch danced just beneath his shoulder blade. A sharp prick raced through him and he tensed.

"Did I hurt you?" She yanked her hands away.

"Don't," he said. "Just the nerves going crazy."

"How many surgeries did you have, Garrett?"

"More than I can count. Skin grafts, shrapnel got embedded into my back. I was a mess."

Her fingers returned to his shoulder blade. "I guess that's what happened here. There's evidence of sutures. It's strange—"

A loud beeping sounded from Garrett's phone. He jumped to his feet. "Get dressed. Someone's broken the perimeter."

Chapter Eight

Laurel rolled off the bed and yanked on her jeans, slipping on her shirt as she raced after Garrett. She followed him out of the bedroom and into his office. He flipped on a switch on one of the consoles. A map flickered to life on the screen. Two green dots headed directly to the center.

"They're getting close to the cameras," he said, turning on another switch. Three monitors buzzed on, the infrared images fuzzy.

A few trees, but nothing more.

Laurel slipped on her shoes and glanced down at the computer monitor where she'd been running the decryption program. "We don't have the password yet," she rushed out. "It hasn't finished. What are we going to do?"

Garrett stared at the monitors. Slowly a figure came into view. She squinted, then recognized a man pushing through the trees, his movements jerky, holding a weapon. A second person followed behind him.

He let out a loud curse. "How did they find us so fast?"

"Who are they?"

"*Not* the family I saw earlier today. There were three of them. And no one was carrying an M16. I could recognize the outline anywhere." Garrett scanned the room and grabbed a duffel from the corner, tossing it toward her. "Pack up what you and Molly need. Only the bare necessities. There's not much time."

At Garrett's grim expression, Laurel's stomach twisted in fear. She raced from the room and quietly opened the door to the bedroom where Molly slept. Using the shard of light piercing through the slit, she fumbled for a few sets of clothes and toiletries. And Ivy's family's picture. Everything else was luxury. Except Mr. Hairy Houdini.

She slipped out of the bedroom and back into the office. "Done."

Garrett sat at one of his monitors. "I'm wiping the entire system. It will disable everything and leave no trace."

"Are they close?"

"They're making a beeline for the cabin, but they're still a half mile away. In the dark in the woods. Idiots."

"Do you recognize them?"

Garrett grabbed a control stick and zoomed in. "No. How about you?"

She squinted at the grainy green image. "I can't tell."

The computer next to her sounded her college fight song. Garrett's eyes widened, and she flushed. "We were…enthusiastic."

She plopped onto the chair. "I've got the password." She typed it in. "I can download it."

Garrett typed in a few commands on his screen. "Copy it. We're out of time."

Two figures appeared on the second screen. This time she could see the second man's gun. Another automatic weapon.

"Military-issue weapons," she said.

"Good eye. They've found us. No telling how many are out there. I'm getting you out of here."

"We should have had another twenty-four hours at least," Laurel said. She looked over at Garrett. "This is my fault."

"Our opponent is better than we both thought."

"Do you have a thumb drive?" Laurel asked.

He opened the drawer and handed her the small device. She stuck the drive into the system, copied the file, then ejected it.

"We're out of time." He grabbed the Remington from a closet, slung the strap over his shoulder and hit a button. The computers started whirring.

"Is it going to explode?" she asked.

"Nothing so *Mission: Impossible,*" Garrett said. "Just wiped clean and its components melted down. Can you carry this?" He lifted up a small backpack.

She took it from him and stuffed it into a duffel, zipping it up. She took her SIG and placed it in the back of her pants. She wished she had a holster. Next time she went on the run, she'd remember to bring one.

"I'll carry Molly." He hurried into the spare bedroom. The little girl had sprawled on her back, clutching her stuffed animal. He slid his hands under her body and lifted her up over his shoulder, settling her on one arm and hip.

"Let's go," he whispered, unclipping a narrow flashlight from his belt. "This has a red filter so it doesn't kill the night vision. I'll lead the way. Keep your weapon handy."

He quietly closed and locked the door behind him. Laurel balanced the duffel on her shoulder. They stepped into the darkness. Only the moon lit their way. He pointed the beam of light at the ground in front of him. "Don't veer off this path. You could walk off a cliff."

Taking it slow but steady, they picked their way through the trees, around a series of rugged rocks, careful not to make any noise. Garrett jostled Molly once and she whimpered. He froze. Laurel held her breath. If Molly started crying she could give their location away.

They started off again.

A burst of gunfire in the distance peppered the night.

Laurel hit the ground. Garrett knelt, covering Molly. She yelped in fear. He placed his hand on her mouth. "Molly, listen to me."

Laurel crawled over to Garrett. "I'm here with you, Molly Magoo. We have to be quiet, even if those noises are scary. Can you do that?"

She nodded her head.

Slowly, Garrett pulled his hand away. Molly slapped her hand on her mouth. "Good girl," he said. "You're very brave."

"Will Santa know?" she asked.

"He's definitely watching."

"Do Mommy and Daddy know?" Molly asked, her voice muffled through her fingertips.

"They're very proud of you, Molly Magoo."

"Lay your head on my shoulder, sugar. We're getting out of here."

Laurel could tell, even in the moonlight, that Molly squeezed her eyes shut.

Another bevy of gunfire erupted.

Garrett didn't slow. "It's at the cabin. Keep moving."

A loud curse pierced the night.

"He said a bad word," Molly muttered. "Santa won't visit his house."

"Definitely not," Garrett said. "Hush now."

They trudged forward. It seemed so much farther back to the SUV than it had hiking up to the ranch house. Laurel focused on the ground in front of her. All she needed was to fall.

She stepped on a twig and the dry wood cracked beneath her weight. Garrett stilled. She stopped, her heart quickening. He motioned her forward.

Laurel didn't know how long they walked before she finally recognized the outcropping of rocks ahead. Garrett paused. Laurel stopped as well, listening to the sounds of the night.

In December, not many animals sounded their call. But neither did the men following.

A twig snapped not that far behind them.

"Go!" he shouted. Placing the keys in her hand, he pushed her through a gap in the rocks. The SUV was just feet away.

"Take her." Garrett shoved Molly into Laurel's arms and took off running in the opposite direction.

GARRETT RACED AWAY from Laurel and Molly. How the hell had these guys found them? He slammed through the pine trees, making as much noise as possible. A gunshot echoed in the night, the bullet hitting a pine tree just above his ear. They had night vision. Great.

Garrett took his flashlight and turned the powerful miniature beam on high, then flipped off the filter, shining the bright light in the direction of the fired shot.

A curse of pain sounded toward him. The guy would be blinded for a few seconds. Garrett veered in the direction of the house. Anything to keep them away from Laurel and Molly. He prayed she'd gotten away, that no one else had intercepted them.

"This way!" one of the men shouted. Footsteps pounded at him. They weren't even trying to be quiet. He took a ninety-degree turn away from the ranch, toward some of the cliffs. He had to keep his bearings. A rock outcropping should be coming up to his right.

Sure enough, the strange formation loomed from the ground.

The men following him kept coming.

The sound of a stumble, then a loud curse, filtered through the night. He hadn't lost them. Garrett rounded the rock formation and paused. Fifteen feet away was the edge of a steep hill, its base jagged rocks. Dangerous, deadly and convenient.

He flipped off his flashlight and raced toward the hill. Those guys trailed after him as though they had radar on him.

Was he carrying a GPS? His phone shouldn't be traceable. How did they have a bead on him? He couldn't hear anything above him; a chopper would be crazy to fly at night in these mountains.

No time to figure it out.

He still couldn't be sure if he wasn't walking into a trap, if someone was waiting for him.

"Laurel, I hope you got away."

He stopped in front of the drop-off. They shouldn't have been able to find him, but the two men barreled into the clearing just in front of him.

The red-filtered flashlight one of them carried crossed his body, and they stopped.

A smile gleamed in the moonlight. "Two years late," the man said, lifting his gun.

Garrett dived to the side just as the man charged. The guy tried to skid to a halt, but momentum carried him over the side. He shouted out and disappeared down the hill.

"Strickland!" the second man shouted. Garrett launched himself at the guy and pinned him. "Who are you?"

The man shook his head.

Garrett shoved the barrel of his Beretta beneath the guy's chin. "I'm not playing games."

"Yeah, well, neither is my boss. I'm dead if I say anything."

The man's eyes were resigned. A bad sign.

"How about we make a deal?" Garrett said, easing the gun just a bit. "You tell me your boss's name. I let you go. You disappear out here. You're a few hours from the border."

A flare of hope flashed on the guy's face before a gunshot sounded. A sharp burning slammed into Garrett's back. His gun dropped from his hand. He rolled off the guy and behind a rock, his back screaming in pain. He sucked in a breath and blinked.

His Beretta lay in the open.

Strickland heaved himself up over the edge of the hill and lifted his M16. "Get out of there, Krauss, or so help me, I'll shoot you, too."

Krauss scrambled away. Staggering toward Garrett, Strickland peppered the rock. Dust and shrapnel flew into the air.

If it had been daylight, Garrett would be dead.

Another blast of firepower and he was running out of time.

"You're dying this time, Bradley. Damn you. Your wife and kid weren't even part of the deal."

The words slammed into Garrett's pain-riddled brain. This son of a bitch had killed his family.

"Yeah, that's right. I set the bomb. You want to come out and face me?"

Garrett rolled over, ignoring the pain in his back. Krauss pulled his weapon. This was a no-win.

Then Krauss moved. Garrett had one chance. With a grunt, he launched himself at Krauss and shoved him into Strickland. Garrett's weight forced them back toward the edge.

They all teetered on the precipice. Garrett grabbed a protrusion of rock and stopped his fall. Strickland and Krauss disappeared over the side.

Garrett could feel warmth seeping down his back as he climbed up the few feet. He flicked on his flashlight and peered over the side.

The men lay against a rock, motionless. Krauss's neck was bent at an unnatural angle, his eyes wide-open. Dead.

Garrett moved the beam over.

Blood covered Strickland's face. He wasn't moving. Garrett pointed his weapon at Strickland, but the guy didn't move. He wanted to climb down, be sure. He needed to know the truth.

A wave of dizziness stopped him. He fell down to his knees. A beeping noise just to his side grabbed his attention. He picked up a tablet. A red dot blinked. It was *him*. Damn it, how were they tracking him?

He pulled everything out of his pockets. He'd bought the clothes in El Paso. It couldn't be them.

He didn't have time to figure it out.

He took one last look over the edge—Strickland still

hadn't budged. Garrett stumbled to his feet. He had to make sure Laurel and Molly were gone, out of here. Daniel would help.

Garrett didn't know how bad his wound was, but he had to make sure they were safe, and then he had to get as far away from them as he could. Because whoever had sent Strickland and Krauss wasn't giving up.

THE GUNSHOTS HAD STOPPED. Laurel gripped her SIG, planting her hands firmly along the hood of the SUV.

Molly sat in the backseat, hugging Mr. Houdini close. "Where is Sheriff Garrett? He wouldn't leave us."

"He'll be here," Laurel said. He had to be here. She chewed on her fingernail.

Suddenly a figure came stumbling out of the trees. Her finger tightened on the trigger.

He looked up at her. "Garrett!" she shouted.

"Get in," he ordered and bounded into the passenger seat. "Drive," he said, clearing his throat.

Carefully she backed up and turned the SUV around. "Lights?" she asked.

"On," he said. "Get us out of here fast."

The beams hit the dirt road and she hit the gas.

"Why the hell did you wait for me? What if I hadn't come back?"

"I have the number you gave me." Laurel gripped the steering wheel. "I was getting ready to call Daniel Adams."

"I don't know whether to be relieved you were here or turn you over my knee." The SUV bounced and Garrett took a sharp intake of breath. Laurel flipped on the interior lights and looked over at him.

His mouth was pinched and the light leather of his seat was streaked with red.

"You're bleeding."

"Just drive," he ordered. "Get to the main road as fast as you can. Maybe we'll be lucky and those two were the only ones following us. For now."

She urged the vehicle forward.

Molly stuck her head between the seats. "Do you need a Band-Aid?" she asked. "I have princess ones. You can have my favorite if you want. Which princess do you like the best?"

Garrett smiled at her. "You're my favorite princess, sugar. And don't you worry. It's just a scratch. I'll be fine."

Laurel's knuckles tightened on the steering wheel. He was lying to protect Molly. Tears stung Laurel's eyes. She'd fallen hard for this man. He'd saved them yet again, but this time she really didn't know if they'd make it out alive. Blood kept seeping onto the seat. She had to get him help.

The nearest town was Trouble. She'd seen a clinic there. She could go back. Everyone knew him there. Someone would help.

It took forever to reach the county road leading to Trouble. She finally got to the intersection.

"Turn left," Garrett said through clenched teeth.

"I'm glad you agree. I'm getting you to a doctor."

"I can't now." Garrett leaned his head back on the seat. "Keep driving straight."

After about fifteen minutes he turned his head to her. In the light of the interior his face had gone pale. "There's a dirt road not too far from here. Pull over and let me out."

"No way—"

"Do it, Laurel."

Against her better judgment, she pulled to the side and stopped the car.

Garrett gripped the door handle and faced her. "Here's what you're going to do. Take this road. It circles down some back roads until you reach Rural Route 11. Follow that until you hit this highway again. Get to a phone, even if you have to buy a prepaid cell at a convenience store. Call Daniel Adams. Tell him what's happening. He'll take you to Covert Technology Confidential in Carder, Texas. They'll protect you."

Daniel's employer might be the only one that could hide Laurel and Molly from the agency and get away with it.

She shook her head. "I won't leave you. You're hurt."

"Laurel, they're tracking me. I don't know how, but they are. You have to get away."

He opened the SUV door, but as soon as his boots hit the pavement he collapsed.

She shoved open her door and ran around the car. "At least let me stop the bleeding before I leave. You can't do it yourself."

He closed his eyes, then gave her a reluctant nod. Why did the thing that attracted her so much to Garrett have to be the very thing that could kill him?

"There's a T-shirt in my backpack. And a canteen. Wash off the wound and use the cotton as a bandage. Then you have to go."

"Are you fixing Sheriff Garrett, Aunt Laurel?"

"That's right, sugar," Garrett said with a smile. "I'll be good as new."

Liar.

Laurel fished out the material and the water. She lifted his shirt and he passed her the flashlight. She gasped. Dried blood caked part of his back, but fresh still oozed from the wound. She didn't know how he was still standing.

She ripped the T-shirt in two and soaked half in water. She bathed his back, trying to be gentle. He didn't even wince.

Each pass removed more of the blood, revealing the scars. They weren't all that bad. The horror of what he'd experienced far surpassed this permanent reminder.

She worked her way toward the area that still bled. The bullet had hit him near his shoulder blade, near where she'd seen his previous wound and stitches. He looked as if he'd scraped his back raw on the rocks, too.

"Just how many times have you been shot in the back?" she asked.

"Since I met you?" he asked. "Or altogether?"

"Wiseass."

"Aunt Laurel, that's a naughty word." Molly gasped.

"Sorry, Molly." She frowned at his back. "See what you made me do?"

He chuckled. "I'm going to miss you two."

She ripped the clean half of the T-shirt for a second round and dabbed at the wound.

He could use stitches, and the raw skin had rocks and metal flakes embedded in it. She had to scrub a bit harder. He sucked in a breath.

"Too bad I still have some feeling left right there," he said, his voice tight with pain.

"Almost done."

As she cleaned the last bit, a familiar-looking object became visible. Small, metallic. A chip.

"Garrett? Were you ever fitted with a tracking device?"

"Hell, no. If the bad guys caught the frequency…" His head whipped around. "Is one back there?"

"Yes."

"Get it out. Now."

"It's implanted in your back. You need a doctor to cut it out."

"Hand me my backpack."

She dug into her duffel. He tugged out the nylon pack and retrieved a small medical kit, complete with a small scalpel and forceps.

"Yank it out," he said. "We don't have any time to lose. They could be closing in now."

Laurel blinked, staring at the tracking device. She could do this. Her hand shook, and she sucked in a deep breath.

"It's easy. You said there was an incision? Just follow the scar and pull the thing out.

"I don't suppose you have pain medicine in your bag of tricks?"

Molly stuck her head over the seat. She gasped. "Sheriff Garrett, you have lots of boo-boos. You can use all my princess Band-Aids if you need them."

"Laurel, just do it." Garrett smiled up at Molly. "Why don't you find me those Band-Aids, sugar?"

Molly ducked behind the backseat.

"Now," he said tightly.

"Brace yourself."

He gripped the passenger seat. She leaned over him. Taking a deep breath, Laurel pushed the knife into his back and sliced the skin, revealing the entire chip. He didn't say a word, but when she grabbed it with the medical tweezers, his back tightened. Blood flowed from the wound.

She dabbed at it. "Got it."

"Oh, yuck. That's a really bad boo-boo."

"Not so bad, sugar. Maybe you'll be a doctor when you grow up so you can fix people."

Molly's smile brightened. "I want to fix people." She hugged her lion tight.

"Laurel, clean the wound with the Betadine. Put some antibiotic ointment on it and use the butterfly strips to close it," he ordered.

Molly insisted on adding several of her own bandages. When they'd finished, Garrett turned to Laurel. His face had gone pale.

"There's a clinic in Trouble," she repeated.

"We can't go back there. Where is the chip?"

She picked up the small device with the forceps. He took it from her and turned it over in his hand. His jawline throbbed. "Damn him."

"Who?"

He lifted his gaze and met hers.

"Your father requested these chips. As far as I knew, they were never used, but he had one put into me. He would have been the only one to know the frequency."

MIKE STRICKLAND GROANED and pressed his hand to his head. It came away bloody and sticky. He rolled over. His entire body hurt. He tested each limb. Nothing broken, though his head might explode at any moment. Slowly he sat up.

Krauss lay next to him, his neck obviously broken. He'd been the weak link anyway. A lot like Derek

Bradley. The guy was a fool. If it had been him, he'd have put a bullet in both men's brains…just to be sure.

Strickland struggled to his feet and glared up the steep incline. "I gotta find that guy."

He searched around. No tracking device. "Damn." He hoped Bradley didn't have it.

A phone sounded a few feet from Strickland. His head pounding as if he had an ice pick stabbed in his ear, he followed the sound and bent down, nearly crying out in pain.

The name on the screen caused his stomach to roil. He vomited all over the ground. He should ignore it.

The ringing stopped, then started again.

"Strickland."

"Don't ignore me again, Strickland."

He wiped his mouth.

"Bradley was moving toward Trouble, Texas, and now his signal has vanished. You failed. Again."

"We have a plan," Strickland lied.

"Oh, really? Now that we can no longer track Derek Bradley, he's an even greater threat. Neutralize him."

"I understand."

"Do you, Strickland? Do you really? Because this is your second mistake in as many days. That's one more than anyone else under my command has made—and still lived."

The phone call ended.

He needed a plan. First to get back to his SUV, and then to find Bradley.

Strickland sank to his knees and emptied the rest of the contents of his stomach next to Krauss's body.

He'd never find Bradley this way.

If he couldn't chase after Bradley, he'd just have to find bait that would attract him.

Trouble, Texas, was the way to do it.

Chapter Nine

Laurel wrenched open the door of the SUV. The destroyed chip lay on the ground, along with her shredded heart. "You're wrong about my father," she said, her face hot with anger. "He would never hurt you like that."

"I know what I saw," Garrett said. "First your sister's evidence pointing to James, and now this."

She scooted into the front seat and gripped the steering wheel. It couldn't be. "He might not have been the perfect father or even around much, but he's a patriot through and through. And he's definitely no traitor."

"Well, neither am I," Garrett snapped. "Yet I'm being hunted. He told lies about me, acted like the heartbroken, betrayed mentor, supposedly to save my life. But now I have to wonder. What better way to hide your true leanings than to throw someone close to you to the wolves and mourn the treason?"

She didn't want to admit the plan sounded good—just simple enough and brilliant enough to have her father's name attached to it. But she wouldn't—*couldn't*—believe James McCallister would do that to Garrett.

"Why did he save your life, then?" Laurel shot back,

desperate to convince him—and herself—that her father hadn't betrayed both of them.

"I haven't figured that out yet."

"If my dad really were responsible for all of this, he wouldn't have kept you alive. He wouldn't have given you your new identity." Laurel put her arm on the back of the seat and faced him. "And Dad sure wouldn't have—" she glanced back at Molly "—caused the explosion in Virginia," she said under her breath.

The little girl's wide eyes went back and forth between them, her lip trembling.

"You're making me cry. I don't like fighting."

Garrett's eyes softened. "Sorry, sugar. Your aunt and I didn't mean to scare you."

Molly hunkered back in the seat, hugging Mr. Houdini close. "Mommy and Daddy fighted about her job all the time."

Laurel twisted in the car. "I didn't know that. What did they say?"

"Daddy wanted Mommy to stay at home with me. I wanted her to stay home, too. Now she'll never stay with me." Molly hugged the stuffed animal and picked at its neck. "She said she was doing something 'portant and couldn't stop them."

"I'm sorry, Molly." Laurel shot Garrett a glare. "We won't fight anymore. Will we?"

He shook his head. "I'm not lying to Molly, because we're going to disagree about this." He gave Molly a small smile. "But, sugar, we'll promise to discuss things more quietly next time. Okay?"

Laurel sighed and started the engine. "Fine. Then

where do we go now? Because I need another look at those files."

"To the next town," Garrett said. "I'll pick up a cell phone."

Still disgruntled, she pressed the accelerator and the SUV took off on the lonely Texas highway. "I still can't believe you, of all people, would assume my father is guilty. They made you out to be a traitor, too."

Garrett didn't say anything at first. "I don't want to believe it. But those chips… James had them developed. He wanted to tag each operative. That way he'd know where they were."

"Seems reasonable. If you were captured—"

"It *was* reasonable, except that we already knew there was a leak in the organization. So he ended the program. No one else had access to the technology, yet I was tagged after the explosion. Now someone is trying to kill us. What would you think?"

"What about the person who designed the chips?" Laurel challenged. "Or the organization that funded the program? My father is ops, not administration."

Garrett stroked his chin, where his beard had grown in since they'd left town. It gave him that outlaw look that Laurel, as a CIA analyst on the run for her life, shouldn't find sexy. But she did.

"Interesting," he said. "I always thought of the killer as ops, but you're right. There are too many layers. That requires redirecting funding and resources. Administrative skills and the ability to hide funding transfers." He drummed his fingers on his knee. "But how do we follow that string to this whole conspiracy?"

"What about Fiona?" Laurel said. "She's got to be

going crazy with James missing, and she'd know who has that kind of power."

"I didn't want to involve her, but we're out of options," Garrett said. "It might be time to bring her in. We're running out of leads. And time."

"And we need someone on the inside, Garrett. You know that." They'd eaten up miles of West Texas roads with not a pair of headlights to be seen. Laurel began to relax. Just a little. Still, they needed communication equipment.

"Let's wait and see if the file has something more." Garrett scanned the pitch-dark horizon. "If not, we'll call her."

"I need access to a computer to look at the file."

"We've gone far enough. Find a place to pull over out of sight. With the chip gone, we should be safe. We'll sleep until daybreak, then head for a public library. That's our best shot of opening Ivy's file."

DARKNESS SURROUNDED THE SUV. A gust of wind shook the vehicle. Garrett shifted his shoulder, seeking relief from the pain. The wound hurt, but he'd had worse. Laurel had rounded the car, slipped into the backseat and cuddled Molly next to her.

She might never forgive him, but what was he supposed to think? Who else could possibly have planted a chip in him after the explosion but James?

Laurel and Molly huddled together, looking less than comfortable, but they couldn't risk going to a motel or even going through stoplights in some of the larger towns. People didn't realize how many cameras watched them. Big Brother really did have an eye on them all the time. Especially when whoever was after him had known his location until a few hours ago. The longer they could stay off the radar, the bigger the search pattern the enemies would require.

And the greater chance of a surprise…if Ivy had found something more than Garrett had discovered when he was doing his digging.

He inched open the door and eased out of the front seat. Laurel had been defiant in defending James. Garrett didn't blame her.

If he hadn't seen Ivy's notes and the telltale design of that chip, he wouldn't have suspected James either. But Laurel was smart and made good points.

Fiona had always had James's back. She'd orchestrated difficult ops with knifelike precision, even those deemed impossible. She almost always found a way for the agents to succeed. She would know *all* the players. Maybe she was the person James had pulled in when he'd told Garrett he was getting close.

Laurel was right. They needed an insider. No matter the risk. He let his gaze rest on her, her eyes shadowed while she tried to sleep. Laurel McCallister was one fierce mama bear when riled. He found that quality strangely attractive. She would need it.

But before he called Fiona, he had to put his backup plan into action. Once he called her, his phone would be tracked.

He dialed a number.

"Adams."

"Daniel. It's Garrett. I definitely need your help."

"Thank God you called. What the hell is going on in Trouble?" Daniel barked like a drill sergeant. "I received a call from your deputy a few minutes ago. I guess he kept my number from our last little adventure.

Evidently he's been taken hostage. Along with Hondo and his sister. The men who took them said he'd better find the sheriff. They left an ultimatum."

"What kind?"

"Come to Trouble. Bring the woman and the girl, but no weapons." Daniel paused. "You have an hour left, Garrett, or they start killing people."

A loud curse exploded from Garrett. "It'll take a majority of that time just to get there."

"Then I'd start driving as soon as you can. I'll meet you there."

Garrett looked through the car's window at Laurel and Molly. Innocent, caught up in a deadly game because of James. Now made worse because of Garrett. That scared the hell out of him. He looked at his watch. He needed a few minutes out of their earshot.

"Daniel, do your *friends* from CTC have contacts in the intelligence community?"

"Oh, yeah."

Garrett cleared his throat. "I need help cleaning up a crime scene. There are two guys at the bottom of Guadalupe Gorge."

"You've been busy."

"There's something else." Garrett paused. "You need to know if you're going to help me. My real name is Derek Bradley."

Daniel didn't say a word, but Garrett could tell from the silence Daniel had heard his name before. "I didn't do what's been said about me. I'm no traitor, but I understand if you decide to back out."

"You don't have to convince me. I've seen you in action. A traitor would have turned his back on me and my wife. A traitor would be living on his own island in the Caribbean, not marking time as a sheriff in a place barely passing for a populated town in West Texas."

A baby's cry sounded in the background. Garrett heard the soft voice of Adams's wife, Raven, speaking to the twins, and then a door closed softly.

"Daniel, think long and hard about Raven and those kids before you commit."

"I am. They'd be dead without you. Besides, I believe you. I've seen what men in power can do to protect themselves." He paused. "I can help you, so shut up and tell me what I need to do."

Garrett let out a long, slow breath and made sure Laurel and Molly were still asleep in the SUV. He walked a few more steps away. "First off, I need protection for two witnesses with a target on their backs. I won't lie, Daniel. It's dangerous."

"Why aren't you going back to your organization? There must be someone there you can trust. Someone whose loyalties you're certain of."

"Maybe one person, but the truth is, I can't tell anymore. The man who saved my life could be keeping me alive as a decoy or a weapon." Garrett hadn't said anything to Laurel, but her father had been the best Garrett had ever seen at deception. A month ago, Garrett would have done anything for James. If his mentor had told him that he'd found evidence of who had killed Garrett's family, he would have exacted justice. Swift and uncompromised justice.

"I don't want anyone at the organization involved," Garrett said, scuffing his boot on the dirt. "I need an independent group that has the contacts to keep Laurel and Molly safe if something happens to me."

"You've got it," Daniel said. "When and where do we meet?"

"No other questions?" Garrett asked.

"Like I said, you saved my life, not to mention my wife and daughters. No questions needed. I know what loyalty means, Garrett. You've earned mine. Now, time is passing quickly. What's your plan?"

"I can't leave my witnesses alone. One is a five-year-old girl. I can't watch them all the time and do what needs to be done."

"I understand," Daniel said. "We'll be there, but it'll take more than the hour you have."

"Then I'll make do until then. I don't know who else will be waiting for us, but meet me in Trouble as soon as you can. I can't let anyone else die because of me."

"Wheels up in ten. See you soon."

THE SUV TURNED a corner, waking Laurel. She blinked her eyes against the hazy light of dawn. She glanced at the back of Garrett's head from the backseat. "You shouldn't be driving. You need rest. And a doctor."

Garrett glanced around at her, then at his watch. "No choice. We're going back to Trouble."

He refocused on the road and pressed down the accelerator, lurching the SUV forward. At the urgency in his actions and his tone, Laurel straightened in her seat. She met his gaze in the rearview mirror. "What's happened?"

"Someone tracking us has taken hostages." Garrett's jaw tightened. "My deputy, Lucy and Hondo. They gave us an hour and time is almost up. They're going to kill the hostages one by one."

"Oh, God." Her hand covered her mouth and she kept her voice low. Molly didn't need to hear this.

"I can't let anything happen to them, Laurel. You understand that."

She nodded, wanting to hold Molly even tighter. This couldn't be happening.

Garrett glanced back at her and Molly. "The problem is, the caller who has the hostages wants all three of us."

"Why? I don't understand. What is it that we've done that's so threatening? Especially Molly?"

"The world thinks we're dead, and we potentially know too much. It's safer and easier to eliminate the witnesses."

"I've seen a lot of evil during my time with the CIA, but this— She's just a little girl." Laurel shivered. "We both know if someone wants you dead, eventually they'll succeed. It's too easy. Tampering with brakes, a car bomb, a sniper shot from a thousand feet away."

"Unless they can't find you." Garrett pressed harder on the gas.

Laurel looked over at Molly. "What's the plan for the three of us?"

"I don't know."

"You're lying."

"I'm running options through my head. It will depend on who is waiting for us, how many. Wish I had a sitrep." The SUV sped up and he glanced at his watch. "They'll call in the next five minutes to set up a rendezvous point. I want to try to surprise them. Hopefully it's not too many."

"I can help, Garrett. I may not have field experience, but I'm a good shot. You know I am."

"You need to protect Molly. I have help coming."

"But will they be here soon enough?"

"I don't know."

"Another lie."

"It's not good that you can read me so easily. I'll have to work on that."

"I'm watching your back, Galloway, so get used to it."

A BRIGHT LIGHT blasted into the midnight-dark prison room. James blinked as the beam burned the backs of his eyes.

He tried to squint through the glare, but he could barely see.

"You should have told us about the chip sooner. It might have saved your daughter Ivy and her family's lives. Too bad she had to start digging and learned too much."

James squeezed his eyes shut tight. God, no. Not Ivy. Not the kids. What had he done? He didn't remember revealing anything, just the shot from a hypodermic needle.

A chuckle from across the room lit a fire of hatred. James jerked up his head, not caring how much it hurt. "You won't get away with this."

"I already have. My reputation is impeccable. I'm trusted. People come to me because they know I'll find a way to get them money, resources, equipment. You knew that, too."

"Which *should* make them suspicious of you."

"People see what they want to see, even in the intelligence community."

His captor pulled out a gun and sauntered over to him. The barrel pressed against his temple. "I should kill you now. You're a loose end."

James knew he wouldn't come out of this alive. For

now, he had to try to get a signal to Garrett. There had to be a way.

"Do it."

"You'd like that. Well, it won't be so easy, James." A quick flick of the wrist brought in a beefy man with eyes cold and dead as a snake. "Find out what else he hasn't told us."

James swallowed. The inflamed scar on the man's face was obviously the result of recent burns. He carried an iron rod with him. "Make it easy. I can't stop until you give me something," the man said, touching his cheek.

The man walked over to a heating element and flicked on a switch. A gas flame roared to life and he stuck the tip of iron in the flames, rotating the bar slowly, evenly. After a few minutes the man pulled the red-hot iron from the flame and walked toward James.

"You don't have to do this," James said. "We could leave together."

He let out a harsh laugh. "I just tried. My daughter was killed in a car *accident* yesterday, along with her boyfriend and two others. I have a wife and son, and I've been told what will happen to them if I fail. I won't try to leave again."

He bent over James. "Now tell me something. Anything. Because I *will* protect my family. Even if you have to die for me to do it."

James closed his eyes. He'd already lost one daughter. Just like this man, he would die to protect Laurel. "I can't."

Scorching heat set fire to his skin. James couldn't stop the scream. Blistering pain, unlike anything he'd ever known.

Suddenly it was gone. James sagged in his chair. He caught his breath.

"Tell me," the man said. "I can't stop."

From outside his prison cell, his captor's words filtered through the bars. "You've arrived? Excellent. Strickland failed twice. You know what to do. Kill Bradley and Strickland. I want this hole plugged up today."

THE BUILDINGS OF Trouble, Texas, were one story and far apart. Dawn had come, and the dim light brought with it visibility. For better or worse.

Garrett couldn't afford to drive any closer on the highway. He turned onto the flat desert plain. "I'm not going in through the main drag. I'll drive through the plains and come in on one of the side streets."

"What about your *friends?*"

"They'll be here soon."

"But not before your meeting." Laurel leaned forward. "You need backup, Garrett. You're one of the walking wounded right now."

She was right, but he had to think of Laurel and Molly first. "You have to watch your niece. She can't afford to lose anyone else."

Laurel hugged the little girl closer.

His cell phone rang.

With a quick movement, Laurel tugged at his wrist. He frowned, but eased the phone from his ear so she could hear.

"Galloway."

"You should have answered *Derek Bradley,*" the voice said. "Traitor."

Garrett cursed under his breath. No one knew about Daniel, so that information had to have come from James.

"I don't know what you're talking about."

"Don't play dumb, *Sheriff.* How close are you to your office?"

"Fifteen minutes."

"Five minutes before I'm scheduled to kill your deputy. You're cutting it close. The poor kid just broke into a sweat."

"I said I'll be there."

"You have the woman with you?"

Garrett didn't respond.

"If I don't have your word that I'll see her outside your office in fifteen minutes, the deputy dies now."

He glanced at Laurel. She nodded.

His lips tightened. "She'll be there."

"And the girl?"

"For God's sake, she's only a child."

A shotgun pump sounded through the phone.

"Damn it. All right, Molly will be there, too."

"Excellent. Look, Sheriff, you play this right, and I *might* let the woman and girl live. But you try to double-cross me and I won't hesitate to kill them. I've done it before." The man paused. "I hear you have a lot of scars from the bomb. Too bad it went off before you were in the car with your wife and kid."

"Strickland? You're dead."

"Guess we're both hard to kill."

The phone went dead.

Garrett's mind whirled. He *still* hadn't killed the bastard. What had he done?

Laurel rested her hand on Garrett's shoulder, but he shook her away.

"Strickland killed my family and I let him leave that ravine." Garrett couldn't think, could barely feel. He'd failed. Again. This time Laurel and Molly might pay the price.

"He won't get away with it," Laurel said. She set her SIG on the front seat. "He killed my family, too. He'll pay. Together, we'll make sure of it."

A BLACK ESCALADE pulled two blocks down from the sheriff's office.

"There's Bradley." Shep Warner looked over at his new partner. Léon had an accent Shep couldn't place, but he had some serious skills. The boss wouldn't have brought him on otherwise. "I worked with him. He was good. Too good, I guess."

"The boss wants him dead."

Shep looked through a pair of Zeiss binoculars. "Someone's in the backseat. Two people. A woman and a kid."

Léon stiffened. "No one said anything about killing a kid."

Shep took a quick image with his camera. "Boss will want to know about this."

He hit Send and waited.

Immediately the phone rang.

"Where did you take this?" The computer-filtered voice always gave him a chill, with its inhuman tone. He had no idea who his boss was, just that his bank account was a lot more robust since he'd started the job. It was just business.

His new partner, Léon, unsettled him. Shep couldn't quite pinpoint what felt wrong. He certainly was a surly bastard, like a robot. Well, if he didn't work out, the boss had a means of making more than one person disappear, particularly when the government had already named anyone missing or disavowed.

"Trouble, Texas. She and a kid are in the target's car."

"Strickland's third strike. Our source here isn't talking. Kill them, too, and dispose of the bodies."

"Won't there be questions?"

"Just make them disappear. In the eyes of the world they are already dead."

Léon turned to Shep. "What's the plan?"

"Leave no one alive. Including Strickland."

"The girl?"

"Even the girl."

Chapter Ten

Two blocks from the sheriff's office, Garrett let the SUV idle. Trouble's Christmas lights knocked against the light poles.

The place looked deserted, causing the hairs on his arms to stand on end. He had a bad feeling about this whole thing. Too many unknowns.

He needed a diversion, and with Daniel and CTC still an hour away, he had no choice about who he had to choose. It tore him apart he'd have to put Laurel in danger.

"We're out of time," Laurel said.

"I know." Garrett let out a sigh. "How's Molly?"

"Resting now." Laurel stroked the girl's forehead. "I gave her some acetaminophen. Her temperature popped up last night, so maybe she'll sleep longer. I need to get her checked out by a doctor."

"Hopefully this will be over soon." Garrett studied the sheriff's office. No one was behind the building. Thank goodness. "I have a way to sneak into the back of the building and get to a stash of weapons, but I need a distraction."

"I'll drive," Laurel said, "and park in front of the

sheriff's office. Hopefully they don't have a bazooka in their arsenal."

"Don't even joke about that, Laurel."

"If I don't joke, I'll run screaming from town, Garrett. I'm terrified for Molly."

He turned in his seat. "And I'm scared for both of you.

"When you hear things go bad in that building, you take off to Hondo's place, the Copper Mine Motel. It was on the right as we headed into town. Daniel will be there soon."

"What about you?"

"If it goes well, I'll get to Hondo, Lucy and the deputy. I'll meet you there with the name of the person who ordered these hits. Let's switch places."

Garrett exited the vehicle, leaving the car running to ward off the nippy morning. He rounded the car and Laurel slipped into the front seat. He knocked on the glass and she cracked the window.

"Give me five minutes before you round the corner. Until then, stay down."

She nodded, but tears glistened in her eyes. "You're a good man, Garrett Galloway, so go kick some bad-guy butt and come back to me."

"I promise I want to." He touched Laurel's cheek, then looked over at Molly. "You're going to do great with her," he said.

Her eyes darkened. "That sounded a lot like goodbye. Please don't let it be."

"You know I need to do this."

"For your family," she whispered.

"And for you." He kissed her lips lightly, lingering for just a moment. "For you and Molly and me."

Garrett eased into the alleyway. He took one last

look at Laurel and lifted up a silent prayer. *Please, let them be okay.* He had to focus on the job at hand: take Strickland out, hope he hadn't brought a ton of friends and save Keller, Hondo and Lucy. Not to mention Laurel and Molly.

He scanned the area. He didn't see anything unusual, then paused. One vehicle stood out. The Escalade had to be Strickland's.

Garrett checked his watch. He didn't have time to hesitate. In less than four minutes Laurel would pull the SUV in front of his building.

He rounded the sheriff's office. He had cameras inside and outside, but they required a password to access. He hadn't even given the code to his deputy. Garrett ran his fingers along the bricks at the back of the building. He pulled out a loose one. Inside was a latch to the emergency entrance. Garrett had always thought the whole setup bordered on paranoia, but now he thanked his overly cautious predecessor. Of course, the man had been right, just not careful enough. He was serving twenty for drug trafficking.

Praying Strickland had kept his deputy in the main room, Garrett entered the digital code and the lock clicked. Slowly he eased the door open.

He heard one set of heavy footsteps pacing from the far room to his left, near the jail cells. Had to be Strickland. He wouldn't allow anyone to be moving around.

"Your sheriff is cutting it close, Deputy," Strickland snapped. The footsteps stopped. "You ready to die for a traitor?"

"Sheriff Galloway is on the up-and-up. I'll never believe he did what you said."

"Damn straight, you cow dung," Hondo hollered, rattling the bars of the cage. "He's twice the man you'll ever be."

Hondo should know better. What the hell was he doing? If Strickland lost his temper, he'd start shooting. Garrett had no doubt that if Strickland had his way, no one would be left alive. Not Laurel or Molly. Not Keller, Lucy or Hondo. And certainly not Garrett.

He glanced at the wall safe, opened it and pulled out an extra set of keys to the jail. If nothing else, he needed to get those keys to Keller or Hondo so they had a prayer of escaping.

A loud clatter rang out. Hondo let out a curse. "You trying to break my hand?"

"Shut up," Strickland said. "Or I'll kill you first. I may choose you anyway. You're too damned annoying."

"No, please, no. Now, Lucy, it's going to be okay."

"Make her stop that sniveling, or I take her." Strickland stomped away, toward the front of the building. "Someone's pulling out front."

That had to be Laurel.

Which meant Strickland had his back to the jail.

Garrett hurried outside the emergency exit to the side of the jail. A small window ledge was the only opening. He lifted himself up, then dangled the keys in front of the glass. He grabbed a diamond cutter from his pocket and within seconds had opened a hole. He set the keys in reach.

Garrett tapped lightly.

Keller jerked his head up. His eyes widened. He sidled over to Hondo. The man slid a subtle glance toward Garrett and gave a nod. At the right moment, they'd grab the keys.

Garrett had to trust the ex-marine to get Keller and

Lucy out safely. He returned to the secret entrance and pushed back inside. The easiest thing would be to shoot Strickland in the back of the head. The man deserved it. Garrett had been dreaming of killing the man since he'd woken up from his coma, but that would silence the only lead Garrett had to the identity of the mastermind behind a decade's worth of death and criminal activity.

And Strickland's death wouldn't protect Laurel and Molly in the long run.

That made his job that much more difficult. He needed Strickland alive, which made his every move that much more dangerous.

Hondo hadn't budged. Good man. Playing it smart. Lucy was tucked up on the end of the cot, rocking away. Easy to see how Strickland had gotten the drop on Hondo. Deputy Keller... Well, Garrett would be having a talk with him.

Strickland held an M16 in his hand. He peered through the front window, stepped aside and opened the door.

"The McCallister woman and the girl. But where's Bradley?" Strickland shifted his M16.

"Guess Bradley didn't believe me when I said one of you would die." He pointed the gun at Lucy.

Now or never.

Garrett launched himself at Strickland, knocking the man's weapon from his hand. Garrett landed on his shoulder and nearly cried out in agony even as he grabbed Strickland by the throat. He pressed his forearm against the man's trachea. "I should have killed you."

Strickland grinned up at him. "But you won't, because

someone will keep coming now that the boss knows you're alive. You can't kill me."

The bastard was right.

Garrett pressed harder, blocking the man's air. "Who do you work for? I want a name."

Strickland glared up at him. "Let me go."

"Let me out. Let me out," Lucy shouted.

Out of the corner of his eye, Garrett saw Hondo pluck the keys from the ledge and unlock the door. Lucy raced from the jail cell the moment Hondo opened it.

With that second's distraction, Strickland thrust his arms against Garrett's chest and twisted his body. He broke Garrett's hold and leaned back just in time to avoid Garrett's killing blow to his windpipe.

Strickland leaped to his feet, grabbed Lucy by the hair and dragged her to the front door.

Garrett raised his Beretta. "You won't get out of here alive."

"Stay still, Lucy," Hondo pleaded with his sister.

The poor woman started crying. Strickland's trigger finger flinched.

"What are you going to do now, Sheriff?" Strickland grinned. "Looks like I'm back in charge. Drop your weapon."

Garrett cursed. He had no choice. He slid his weapon over.

Keller circled around Strickland. The man didn't hesitate. He let a bullet fly. Keller went down, his shoulder bloody.

"No more games. Get McCallister and the girl inside, and we'll finish this."

Before the words left his mouth a gunshot echoed through the room.

Lucy screamed.

Strickland fell to the floor, unmoving.

Hondo ran to his sister and cradled her in his arms, turning her away from the dead body. "I was only bringing the deputy cookies," she babbled.

"Everyone down." Garrett raced to the open front door. He stood in the doorway, Beretta drawn. Molly was ducked down in the backseat. Laurel had squeezed under the SUV. "He's dead," Garrett said.

Laurel's eyes widened; she crawled toward him, rose and threw herself into his arms.

"Did he say anything?" she whispered. "Give us any information?"

Slowly Garrett shook his head. "I'm sorry."

"I understand."

But her voice held a resignation that Garrett didn't like. She, too, realized the implications. If Ivy's file didn't give them the name of the person responsible, they were at a dead end. That could cost all three of them their lives.

THE BLACK ESCALADE backed out of sight of the sheriff's office. Shep shoved the gear into Park and glared at Léon. "You should have taken the shot. Strickland was easy, but Bradley was in your sights twice. First when he orchestrated that harebrained scheme with the keys, then through the front door. You could have taken them both out."

His new partner shook his head. "The deputy would have been collateral damage. Plus, I saw movement inside through that front window."

"So what?"

"The boss doesn't want too many bodies that can't be explained. I need to be able to take them out quick, and we have to move in and grab them…or they need to disappear."

"I didn't hear that order."

"Well, I was told when I was brought on board to keep every job out of the papers and low-key. Killing a bunch of people in a sheriff's office will make the news. Trust me, that's how the boss wants it."

"Then how do you expect to get the job done?" Shep asked. This new guy was really starting to bug him. And his accent irritated the hell out of Shep.

"I've got an explosive in the back of the truck that makes C-4 look like Play-Doh. Nothing for forensics to find. We follow them, get them together, blow the car and leave. It'll burn so hot nothing is left. It's cleaner. And we get rid of them all at once."

Shep drummed his fingers on the dash. "Explosives. That's why the boss brought you in. Léon, I may like your style after all."

"Then we're in agreement." Léon peered through his binoculars. "Hmm…looks like we won't have to make Strickland disappear. Our friendly neighborhood deputy's hiding the body."

"Maybe he's taking it to the morgue."

Léon shook his head. "Wrapped the guy in a blanket and dumped him in a pickup. They're getting rid of the body."

"One less task for us to finish."

"One more reason to do this job right, because I refuse to be made into an example of my new boss's desire for perfection."

HONDO'S MOTEL ROOMS were simple, but comfortable. Laurel took a long, slow breath, but her nerves refused to settle. At least the chaos from outside had disappeared.

The group of CTC operatives who had arrived had taken over the motel and the sheriff's office and pretty much secured the entire town. No one went in or out without CTC knowing it.

They'd searched for the man who'd shot Strickland, but the only lead was an unfamiliar black Escalade that had raced out of town. An expensive car carrying a sniper with a good eye.

They'd be back.

Laurel couldn't feel completely safe, even with the armed guards at the door. The two men originally tailing her might be dead, but they'd been replaced. Someone wanted her, Molly and Garrett dead, not to mention they still hadn't heard from her father.

Laurel shifted backward and let her spine rest against the bed's headboard. Molly crawled into her lap, resting against her chest. With a sigh, Laurel hummed the addictive ant song Garrett had sung the night before.

Everything around this room seemed peaceful and safe, but Laurel could feel the tension knotting at the back of her neck. Her gut urged her to run, but she had nowhere to go.

She had to trust Garrett and his friends.

Molly picked at Mr. Houdini, rocking him slightly. She'd gone way too quiet after the latest attack. Would Molly ever be the same? Laurel knew she wouldn't.

Molly snuggled closer and squeezed her lion tightly, playing with its collar.

A knock sounded at the door. Molly jerked in Laurel's arms as the door opened. Laurel palmed her SIG and aimed it at the woman with black hair who stood on the motel's porch. Behind her, Laurel recognized one of the CTC operatives standing guard.

"Who are you?" she asked.

"Raven Adams, Daniel's wife. May I come in?"

The man Garrett trusted so much. One more leap of faith.

Laurel nodded and lowered the SIG, but kept it within reach.

A large reddish-colored dog panted beside Raven. "How about my furry friend, Trouble?" She tilted her head toward her canine companion.

Molly straightened a bit in Laurel's lap and stared closely at the dog, which seemed to smile.

"Come in," Laurel said.

The moment Raven crossed the threshold, Trouble bounded toward Molly, but he didn't jump on the bed. He simply tilted his head and stared at the little girl, then put his big head down on the bed and looked up at Molly with sad brown eyes.

"Your dog's name is Trouble?" Laurel asked.

Raven smiled. "It's a long story. He gets more people out of trouble than into trouble, though."

Molly bit her lip and scooted off of Laurel's lap. "Can I pet him?"

"He'd like that," Raven said. "He especially likes getting his ears rubbed."

Molly reached out a tentative hand and patted Trouble's head. The dog's tail thumped.

"He likes me," Molly said. She moved her fingers to his ears and scratched. The big dog leaned into her and practically groaned with pleasure.

Molly slid off the bed. "He's big." Her lion in one arm,

she wrapped her other around the big dog and hugged him. "I like you."

Raven held up a bag. "Have you had some of Hondo's cookies? He likes you a lot, Molly, so he gave me a few cookies just for you."

Molly's ears perked up even as she rubbed Trouble's nose. "Chocolate chip?"

"Is there another kind of cookie?" Raven opened the bag and passed a cookie to Molly. "Daniel and I wanted to invite Molly to take a ride on a plane and visit my house. I have a swing set in the backyard. It's too big for my little girls, but it might be just Molly's size."

Trouble rolled onto his back and Molly giggled, rubbing the dog's belly. The smile that lit her eyes made Laurel's heart ache.

"She'd be safe with us," Raven said.

Laurel leaned down and patted Trouble. Then she stroked Molly's hair. "When are you leaving?"

"Daniel and Garrett are discussing their plans."

"Really?" Laurel crouched down in front of her niece. "Molly Magoo, I need to go speak with Sheriff Garrett. Do you want to stay here with Trouble?"

Molly nodded.

"Do you mind watching her for a few minutes?" Laurel asked Raven. "She's had a rough time. If she needs me, I'll be right outside."

Laurel started toward the door. Raven took one of Laurel's hands. "You can trust Garrett. He's one of the good ones."

Laurel studied the woman's eyes and recognized the tortured memories of events gone by. Raven had seen things. Laurel looked back at Molly.

"I'll take good care of her. I almost lost my girls. I

don't take their safety for granted." Laurel hesitated. "Look, I know you don't know me from any woman off the street, but Garrett and Daniel saved my life and the lives of my children. There's no one else I'd want in my corner if I were facing the devil himself."

Laurel met Raven's gaze. "We're in a lot of trouble. What if it follows Molly to you?"

"More of Daniel's organization will be stationed at my house. She'll be well guarded. And Trouble will be there, too."

Laurel bit her lip. "I'll think about it."

She walked out of the motel room. Several men with serious faces and equally impressive weapons prowled the area. One tipped his cowboy hat at her. "Ma'am. The sheriff's in the next room over."

Laurel walked in. Garrett sat next to Daniel Adams at a small table near the window, studying the screen of a laptop, deep in conversation.

She strode over to them. "What have you found out from Ivy's information?"

Garrett lifted his head, but the guilt in his eyes gave him away. "We should talk about this later."

"I don't like the secrets," Laurel insisted. "Tell me."

He turned the laptop around and Laurel read through the first page. "This can't be true."

"Ivy's file makes a direct connection between your father and almost every agency leak. It connects gun running, selling of top secret documents and the movement of over a billion dollars into overseas accounts."

Laurel snatched the laptop from him and sat on the bed. She took in page after page. Her shoulders tensed at each new, damning word. "I don't believe Ivy wrote this." Laurel raised her gaze to meet Garrett's. "This is the file I downloaded?"

Garrett nodded.

"She's wrong. She has to be. If anyone saw this—"

"Your father would be convicted of treason."

"He wouldn't do any of this. And I'm not just being naive." She lifted her chin and stared at Garrett.

He knelt beside the bed and held her hand in his. "I don't think so either, but I do believe someone else within the agency is setting him up. Just like me."

"What can we do? Strickland is dead."

Daniel cleared his throat. "After I spoke with Ransom Grainger, the head of CTC, about you, he let me in on some sensitive information. CTC has a contact buried deep in a covert operation within the agency. Ransom had been asked to investigate some irregularities within their overseas operations," he said.

"By who?"

"Let's just say it's someone at the very highest levels of the government. There was a whistle-blower involved."

"Who?" Laurel asked.

"James McCallister."

"Dad?"

"I think this is why he hoped to solve my case," Garrett said.

"Daniel, can you help us identify who wants us dead? Maybe even find out what happened to my father?" Laurel asked. "Can CTC?"

The CTC operative frowned. "Our informant hasn't met face-to-face with the highest level in the organization yet. Evidently, whoever's in charge keeps things very secret, so it's delicate. Any contact with our operative and we risk his life. Too many questions and he'll disappear. Others have."

"So, what do we do until then?" Laurel asked, rubbing the back of her neck to try to get rid of the headache threatening to escalate into agony. "Eventually that sniper will find a way to us. We can't hide forever."

Garrett rose and looked down at her, his expression warning her she wouldn't like whatever he was going to say. "That's why I want you and Molly to disappear for a while with Daniel and Raven."

Laurel took in Garrett's grim face. "You'll come with us, though. You're in danger, too."

"I can't, Laurel. I'm going to—"

"Get yourself killed," Laurel finished.

"I think I'll leave you two to hash this out." Daniel disappeared out the door, closing it behind him.

Garrett plucked the laptop from her and brought her to her feet. He touched her cheek. "I'm going to find James and take this guy down, but I can't focus on the mission if I'm worried about you and Molly. I don't want you hurt, Laurel. Your father would want you out of the cross fire."

"That's playing dirty." She scowled at him, knowing exactly what he was doing and hating him for it.

"I'm telling the truth." He bent down and gently touched her lips with his own. "It has to be this way. For Molly. You know that."

Garrett laced his fingers with hers. She liked the way they intertwined, as if they were one. They'd known each other just a few days, and yet she felt as if they'd been together always. She didn't want to lose him.

"I don't like it."

"But you'll do it." Garrett squeezed her fingers. "For Molly."

"For Molly."

With a soft peck on her lips, he walked to the door and opened it. "Daniel, I need transportation."

Daniel slipped a phone from his pocket. "To D.C.?"

"That's where this thing started. That's where I'll end it."

"Give me a couple of hours to get a plane here. You guys have been up all night. Rest. We'll take care of things for a while."

"Thanks, Daniel. I owe you."

"We're even now," he said. "I'm going to find my wife."

Daniel closed the door on them and Garrett faced Laurel. She could hardly breathe. "I don't like this. It feels wrong. I came to you. I caused you to lose everything."

Without hesitation, Garrett tugged her back into his arms. "You're wrong. You brought me back to life, Laurel."

He stroked her arms, warming the chill that had settled all around her with the knowledge that this might be the last time he held her.

"I'm afraid. For you."

"All I want is for you to be safe. That's all James would want. This is your chance."

She could barely breathe. "Hold me, Garrett. Tight. Please."

"I'll do more than that." Garrett lowered his lips to hers and pressed them open.

With a low groan she wrapped her arms around his waist, pressing her ear to his chest, listening to the strong beat of his heart, memorizing his scent, the feel of him, taking in every moment, terrified that soon it would be over. Soon he would be gone and she would have only this moment to cherish.

When Garrett pulled back slightly, she couldn't stop the moan of protest. But he didn't let her go. He cupped her face this time, the kiss so very sweet, so very loving. So very scary. Like a goodbye.

Without words, he scooped her into his arms and laid her down on the bed, spooning against her back.

He threaded his fingers with hers, breathing in deeply. "If things were different, I would take you away. I would disappear with you. Believe that."

She brought his hand to her chest and squeezed tight. "I'm terrified. For you. For my father. So many people have died." Laurel turned in his arms and touched his cheek, taking in each line of tension, each fleck of gold in his brown eyes. "I don't want to lose you now that I've found you."

"I'll do everything I can to bring your father home, Laurel."

"And you, too. I want you back, Garrett." She clutched the front of his shirt. "You made me feel something these last few days. I've always believed I could only rely on myself. My father taught me that. But you— I feel like I can count on you. I want and need you in my life. Don't die on me."

"I have a whole lot to live for these days," he said softly. "I don't want to leave you." He pulled her closer, and she realized he'd never made a promise that he'd come back. For the first time, the easy lie didn't trip off his lips.

She felt the truth in every word.

GARRETT WATCHED LAUREL sleep for two hours. The rise and fall of her chest, the gentle smile on her face. He wanted nothing more than to take her away and make a new life for all of them, but he knew better. This would never be over, Laurel and Molly would never be safe, his family and Laurel's family would never be avenged until the traitor in the organization was stopped.

Garrett had said goodbye with every kiss, every touch, every caress. Knowing it might be for the last time, he slipped out of the bed with a sigh, pulled on his boots and walked out of the room.

Laurel wouldn't be surprised to awaken and find him gone, but she'd be furious. He knew they were lucky to have survived the past few days. Luck didn't last forever.

He closed the door quietly. Daniel stood on the porch of the Copper Mine Motel in a small pool of sunlight, Raven folded in his arms, a blanket wrapped around her.

Several armed guards nodded at them. Daniel nodded back.

"Any strangers in town?"

"None. And no sign of the Escalade. It looks clear. For now."

"And Molly?"

"Playing on my tablet, using Trouble as a pillow," Raven said with a smile. "She's a tough little thing. Not to mention a girl after my own heart, with her fondness for Hondo's chocolate-chip cookies."

"How are Hondo and Lucy? And Keller?"

Daniel frowned. "Lucy isn't handling it well. Doc gave her a sedative. Keller's going to recover, but he's got a lot of questions."

"Poor Lucy. She's been through hell. You know, I spent the last year in this town playing the waiting game when I wanted to be in the action. Now I've hurt the people who gave me their trust when they shouldn't have. I don't know how to make it up to them."

"You can catch whoever's responsible and make them pay." Hondo's harsh voice came from around the corner. The big man looked devastated.

"Hondo." Garrett stilled. "I'm so sorry about you and Lucy—"

The motel owner raised his hand. "You didn't bring them here. They came after you. Lucy knows better than anyone that evil exists. Her ex-husband's beatings damaged her brain and left her with a childlike innocence. Then a few months ago she was shot and nearly killed. She sees the truth now, though." Hondo handed over another bag of cookies. "Give these to Molly. Lucy wants her to have them. She wouldn't let herself sleep until I brought them out here."

"Again, I'm so sorry."

"Sheriff, you want to make it up to me? Take care of those men, then come back. Obviously Trouble needs a lawman who knows how to handle more than just old man Crowley's drinking binges. We need good men around here, and that's what you are. So get it done."

Hondo disappeared back behind the screen door, then closed and locked it.

Garrett exhaled slowly, shoved his hands into his pockets and looked at Daniel. "I left everything I know about this case on a disk in the top drawer in the hotel room. If I don't come back…use your best judgment."

Daniel nodded.

"Strickland and Krauss are gone, but there are more coming." Garrett pulled Strickland's phone from the evidence bag. "Once I turn this on, sooner or later someone will track it, or the traitor at the other end will call."

With a solemn nod, Daniel rubbed the back of his neck. "Then press the button and let's get this damned thing over with."

GARRETT DROVE THE TRUCK several hours from Trouble before he pulled off to the side of the road. He didn't want anyone being led to Laurel.

He dozed, dreaming of lying next to Laurel and cuddling her warm body with his. Afternoon sunshine filtered into the pickup. The phone hadn't revealed the blocked number, so his only choice had been to wait for the call. He'd signaled Daniel with a text, and CTC would triangulate the signal.

Just past twelve-thirty the phone rang.

"Derek Bradley, I assume?"

Garrett immediately texted Daniel: The tracking began.

"Strickland and Krauss are dead, I understand. That must feel good, Mr. Bradley, considering Strickland blew up your family right in front of you."

"Not particularly. But then again, I don't get off on killing people."

"Should I even ask what you want, Mr. Bradley? Or should I call you Garrett?"

"A bargain. For the lives of Laurel McCallister and Molly Deerfield. They walk away. No one follows them and they're left alone."

More silence, and a prickle of unease rocked down Garrett's spine.

"That could be possible. Ivy Deerfield was a better detective than you were, Garrett. She infiltrated my organization farther than I would have expected. She collected information I wish returned to me. Returned and destroyed."

"I have her evidence." Garrett waited for several moments. He had to keep the traitor on the phone.

"Your proposition has merit."

Interesting. Whoever was on the other end of the phone felt vulnerable.

"I can come to you," Garrett offered.

"It may very well be time we meet. Then you might begin to understand."

Anticipation coursed through Garrett's blood. He knew he was walking into a trap.

It didn't matter.

"Tell your friends that their attempt to triangulate my location won't work. Besides, you don't have to guess where I'll be, Sheriff. Come to James McCallister's home. Alone. It's a fitting spot for our…reunion. You have until midnight tonight to be here. Or I *will* finish my original plan and eliminate Laurel McCallister and her niece."

Chapter Eleven

Laurel awakened without warmth next to her. She stretched her palm across the motel-room bed, but the sheets were cool to the touch. She didn't have to call out to know Garrett was gone.

Keep him safe.

The silent prayer filtered through her mind. She tucked her legs up. Her skills hadn't brought them the answer. Ivy's investigation had done nothing but incriminate their father, just as he seemed to have done to Garrett. Which was probably why Ivy had thought about leaving the organization.

Garrett would never stop trying to prove his innocence and avenge his wife and daughter, though. And he wouldn't stop now to protect her and Molly.

He was that kind of man. A hero, but the kind of man who could get himself killed in the name of justice.

There had to be something they were missing. That Ivy had missed.

Laurel sat up and rubbed her eyes. How long had she been out?

She slipped on her shoes and opened the door. Daniel stood near her room, his body watchful, his weapon at his side.

"Molly?"

"With Raven and Trouble next door. She's fine."

"I need to see her," Laurel said.

"Sure thing." Daniel took a scan around and met the gaze of a CTC operative at the other end of the motel. "Go on."

Laurel rushed the five feet to the next room and opened the door.

"Aunt Laurel!" Molly grinned, gave Trouble a pat, grabbed her stuffed lion and raced over. "Trouble and me are bestest friends now. Can I have a dog like him? I'll take good care of him and feed him and give him water, and take him for walks, and pick up his poop." She wrinkled her nose. "If I have to. Miss Raven said you were resting. I'm glad you're done. Where's Sheriff Garrett?"

Raven sat cross-legged, hosting a makeshift picnic on the bed.

Laurel fingered Molly's blond hair, able to breathe for a moment, knowing her niece was safe. "He left, Molly Magoo."

Everything within Laurel longed to assure Molly that Garrett would be back soon, but the words simply wouldn't come. Laurel not only couldn't be certain; she feared the worst.

Molly stilled; a frown tugged at the corners of her lips. "He didn't even say goodbye. That's not polite. And I wanted to show him my star. I kept forgetting before. It's just like his when we first met him."

"You have a star?" Laurel asked in confusion.

"Mommy put it on my lion."

Molly held out Mr. Houdini. Laurel stared at the small charm hanging from the lion's collar. She dug into her pocket and retrieved the charm bracelet that her father had sent to Ivy. No charms were missing from it. Every other silver shape had meaning—a seashell representing the last vacation with their mother, a horse for when they'd learned to ride, a ballerina from the terrifying lessons both girls had endured before their mother let them quit.

But a sheriff's star. It had no meaning in their lives. Except in reference to Garrett.

"When did she put this on, Molly?"

Molly's forehead crinkled in thought. "The day I got sick. She said it was a special star. Grandpa sent it and I had to protect it 'cause I was a brave girl just like the man who wore the star. That's Sheriff Garrett, right?"

"Yes, I think it is." Laurel could barely speak past the thickening of her throat. "Can I borrow it, honey?"

Her niece's face went solemn. "You'll give it back?"

"I promise, Molly Magoo."

Laurel slipped off the lion's collar and returned the animal. She opened the door and motioned Daniel over. "Do you have a magnifying glass or a microscope?"

Daniel's brow rose. "What's up?"

"Maybe nothing. Maybe an answer."

Daniel rounded the back of one of the black vehicles swarmed in the motel's parking lot. He dug into a duffel bag in the back. "Raven is always telling me I carry weird stuff in my bag." He handed her a small magnifying glass. "I've had it since I was a kid. My father taught me to build fires with it."

Laurel sat down at the table in the motel room and laid the charm down. She studied it closely. Molly had carried that lion everywhere. She'd almost left it behind in Virginia when'd they run that very first night.

After studying one side and seeing nothing, she gently turned it over and there it was.

"A microdot." She looked up at Daniel. "We have to find out what's on it, fast. It could save Garrett. And my father."

LAUREL SAT CROSS-LEGGED on the bed, staring at the computer file that the CTC technicians had pulled from the microdot.

Page after page of all the proof she needed that Garrett and her father were innocent. Except for one thing— the true identity of who was behind all the transactions.

But why had her father and Ivy kept it secret?

"Oh, Ivy, where do I go from here? Who were you going to give this to? If only Garrett were here. He might see something unusual."

She opened the motel-room door and called out to Daniel. "Any word yet?"

He shook his head. "They haven't broken radio silence. They will as soon as they can. All I can confirm is that they landed in D.C. a few hours ago."

"D.C.? No. Garrett's walking into a trap." She frowned at Daniel. "You know that."

Worry creased Daniel's forehead. "You have to trust him. I've looked into who Garrett used to be. The man was very good at his job."

Laurel scrubbed her face. This wasn't the same situation. He was a known traitor to the rest of the world. The moment law enforcement recognized he was alive, if someone killed him, not that many questions would be asked.

The answer was in that file. Laurel had to decipher

it. She had to save him somehow. She needed someone who could help her see what she was missing.

She closed the door on Daniel and paced the motel room. She wanted him here, with her. Safe. She longed for him to hold her in his arms, to talk this over with him. She had to call in her last resort.

She toyed with the phone in her hand. Garrett had wanted to keep Fiona out of it, but with the new information from the microdot, Fiona might be the only other person who could help. She could put the word out Garrett was innocent, and that her father was innocent. Save their lives.

Maybe even help Laurel decipher something hidden in the file—something Ivy and James had known about, but that Laurel couldn't identify. Then Garrett wouldn't have to go through with whatever risky plan he and his CTC friends had come up with.

Her finger paused over the numbers. Garrett hadn't wanted to trust anyone else, but even he had recognized Fiona's knowledge. With a deep breath, Laurel dialed Fiona's personal number. No way Laurel could risk her call being recorded.

"Fiona Wylde." The woman's voice was pleasant, welcoming. As it always was. This woman could very well marry her father someday.

"Fiona, it's Laurel."

The woman gasped. "But…I thought… Oh, my God, James and I thought you were dead."

Laurel's knees buckled and she sagged onto the bed. "You've seen my father. Is he okay? Is he safe? I've been so worried about him."

"Oh, honey." A sob came through Fiona's voice. "He's been through hell, but he escaped yesterday and found his way home. We thought..." She could barely choke out the words. "We thought we'd lost everyone."

Laurel's hands trembled. "Can I...can I talk to him?"

"Of course." Laurel heard fierce whispering in the room. "I'll put it on speakerphone. His hands...have been injured. He's weak, but it's all okay now."

"L-Laurel?"

Her father's voice sounded tired, hoarse.

"Dad. Oh, Dad. You're okay?"

"I've been better." He let out a chuckle, then started coughing.

"I have proof you aren't a traitor, Dad. And neither is Garrett."

"But how?" Fiona asked. "We've been trying for so long. I thought we'd have to leave the country. I couldn't find anything but horrible corroboration that your father was dealing with terrorists."

"I-Ivy. You know what happened—?"

Fiona cut Laurel off. "I'm so sorry, Laurel. Look, your father is hurt. Badly. And he has to lie down, but we need to talk—"

A grunt sounded through the phone, then a crash.

"James!" Fiona shouted. "Laurel, your father just fell. I have to go to him." Muffled whispers filtered through the receiver. "James, darling, stay still. You've torn the stitches."

The phone went silent. Laurel gripped the cell tight. "Fiona, is Dad okay?"

"For now. I've had to treat him myself." Worry laced Fiona's breathless voice.

"Garrett Galloway is going to Washington. He needs help. Please."

"I have to get back to your father. I don't know what

I can do. We felt it better to keep James's reappearance and Galloway's identity a secret. I could make it worse. Things don't look good at the agency."

"But if you looked at the file, maybe we can discover who is doing this."

"You have the file? With you?"

"Yes. Please, Fiona."

"Don't send it to me," she said sharply, all business now. "Come to his house, Laurel. I have someone I trust who can bring you. Are you still in the U.S.?"

Laurel took in a deep breath. "I'm in Texas."

"What are you doing—? Oh, Garrett."

"You knew about him?"

"Of course. James and I share everything. But we had to keep it quiet."

"I wish I'd known."

"I understand. Listen to me, Laurel. I *have* to get off this phone. It's been almost three minutes. We can't risk surveillance. I'll send a plane for you. Your father needs to see you." She lowered her voice. "And, Laurel, don't tell anyone where you're going. Anyone. Do you understand? Not until we end this. Once and for all. Trust no one but me."

THE BLACK ESCALADE idled on the side of the road. Shep glared at Léon. "You got us lost. Do you know what the boss does to people who make mistakes?"

"I watched you blow Strickland's head off," Léon snapped. "I get the picture."

"We should have taken out the woman and girl first?"

Léon fiddled with the GPS receiver. "Do I need to explain this in small words, Shep? Galloway's the hard target. We kill him first. He's the biggest risk."

Shep thrust his fingers through his hair. "Well, we're pretty close to finding him right now, aren't we?"

The device in Léon's lap beeped. He smiled. "Maybe I just saved the day."

The tablet blinked on again. Shep let out a curse. "Are you going to be able to fix that thing or not?"

Léon tugged out a small tool set. "I'll fix it. Be patient."

"Tell that to the boss."

The phone sitting between the two men rang.

"Are we bugged?" Shep pressed the speakerphone button. "Yeah, boss?"

"I have a job for you."

"Kill our three targets and dispose of the bodies," Shep repeated.

"No. I want you to pick up your targets just outside of Trouble, Texas, and bring them to me. I'll give you the location."

"We could dispose of them more easily here."

"Are you questioning me, Shep? Strickland started using his brain—that's why you had to blow it away."

"Of course not."

The boss rattled off a rendezvous point. "I want them both alive. I need them unharmed. At least for another few hours." There was a slight pause. "After that, you can use them as target practice."

JAMES MCCALLISTER'S VIRGINIA home appeared deserted.

Garrett glanced at his watch one more time. Five minutes to midnight. He looked over his shoulder. Rafe had parked a second vehicle down the block. They both recognized this was a trap, but they also knew it was important that the mastermind behind this plot believe Garrett had come alone.

He'd taken every precaution he could, because he wanted to survive. He wanted to see if what he'd experienced with Laurel was real. It felt real—almost too good to be true, which made Garrett distrust it all the more—but, oh, how he wanted it to be real.

He'd never thought he could love anyone again, not after his heart had been destroyed when he'd lost Lisa and Ella, but Laurel had put her faith in him, despite the doubts that had to have raced through her mind more than once since they'd met.

They hadn't known each other long, but Garrett had been dead inside long enough to know what he felt. He had two very good reasons to make it out of this op alive.

He glanced at his watch. One minute before the agreed-upon time.

Garrett slammed the door on the vehicle and walked up the concrete sidewalk. When he reached the familiar front porch he hesitated. He might never come out. And he hadn't told Laurel how he felt. He'd tried to show her, but he hadn't been able to say the words. If he died tonight, he didn't want the words haunting her, but right now he wished he'd said something. He prayed she knew how special she was, how much she deserved to be loved with all a man's heart and soul.

He wanted her to know what was between them meant something more than two people seeking comfort. She truly was an amazing woman, and he wanted to see her again. He wanted to tell her he loved her.

Garrett pressed his finger on the doorbell.

The front door slowly opened. His shoulders tightened. Silence greeted him from the house. He stepped inside. Behind the door, tears streaming down her face, Laurel McCallister had let him in.

"What the hell are you doing here?" Garrett reached out to her, but Laurel stepped back.

"I invited her."

Garrett turned around.

"Fiona?"

Fiona Wylde. James's lover. A woman he knew well. Strike that. Based on the gun she had drawn on him, Fiona was a woman he'd *thought* he knew well.

"You're a difficult man to kill." She nodded at a man standing in the shadows. "Disarm him, Léon."

A man gave a quick nod. He walked over to Garrett, patted him down and removed the Beretta from his back, the knife from his ankle holster and the small pistol hidden within his boot.

Léon met Garrett's gaze and patted his other boot, right over where a second knife was hidden. What the hell?

"Cuff him and bring them both downstairs. We'll have a family reunion."

Garrett slid a glance over at Laurel. "Damn it. Why are you here?" She was supposed to be safe, with Daniel, with CTC.

"I found a microdot Ivy left. It contains proof of your innocence and my father's, too," she said, her gaze resigned. "I called Fiona thinking she'd help us."

"Oh, darlings, after tonight, you'll never have to worry again." Fiona led them down to the basement. She hit a code in a panel on the concrete wall. A door to a small room opened up.

James McCallister sat slumped over in a chair, his arms and legs tied in place. He couldn't lift his head.

Garrett saw the flicker of James's eyes, but his clothes

were in tatters, his face bruised. Burns smoldered his pants.

"Dad," Laurel shouted.

"Aunt Laurel?" Molly's cries sounded from behind a door. "Let me out! Please, let me out!"

"Tie them to the chairs," Fiona ordered. "We end this today."

Léon shoved Garrett toward a steel chair and pushed down on his head, indicating for him to sit. The man took nylon rope and secured his hands and feet. A second man did the same to Laurel.

"Why do this, Fiona?" Garrett asked, clenching his muscles against the ropes. He needed room to work if he was going to escape and get Laurel, Molly and James to safety.

"I'm not having a reveal-my-inner-motivations conversation with you, Garrett, because there are none. I'll make it simple. I did it for the money. A *lot* of money."

"He's secure," Léon said. "What about the little girl in the closet?"

"Leave her."

Fiona stalked up the stairs, then whirled around. "I don't want any evidence left behind. Everyone in that room is dead or missing. They aren't to be found." She paused. "And, Léon, this is why I smuggled you into the country. Those explosives should take the house down. Get it down so it's too hot to find even a fragment of bone."

"Where's your loyalty?" Laurel shouted. "To my father, if no one else. He loved you."

"Ah, love and loyalty. How quaint. Almost as heartwarming as Léon's amusing use of handcuffs." Fiona looked down from her perch on the stairs. Her eyes hardened. "Haven't you learned there is no loyalty? The powerful feed off the powerful. And heroes die for nothing. The only thing you have is yourself and your needs. You should have remembered that, Laurel."

Léon and his friend followed Fiona up the stairs. The door closed behind them.

Garrett palmed the key that Léon had placed in his hand. Twisting his wrists, he maneuvered free of the handcuffs, then pulled out of his other boot the knife... the one Léon had left.

Laurel stared at him. "How?"

"Daniel's inside guy. We don't have much time."

Garrett cut through the zip ties around Laurel's wrists. She ran to the door.

"I'm here, Molly."

"Aunt Laurel, help me!"

She tugged on the doorknob. Locked.

"Molly, step back from the door, honey. Hide in the corner."

Garrett gave the lock a hard kick and the door broke free. Laurel scooped up Molly.

"I'll get your father," Garrett said.

Above them an explosion roared. Glass shattered; timbers fell. Laurel raced up the stairs and put her hand on the door. "Fire. Smoke's starting to come through. We're trapped."

"If Léon set the charges, I hope to God he gave us extra time." Garrett knelt in front of James and shook him. "Tell me you followed your own advice, old man. Where's the escape route out of here?"

Laurel hurried down the stairs.

"James, we don't have much time."

The old man blinked. "Behind their mom's picture." His voice croaked.

Garrett spun around, but he didn't see a painting of a woman on the wall. "Where is your mother's picture, Laurel?"

"There's only the mural she painted."

The starry night sky covered one wall.

Murky smoke began to filter into the room. "Get washcloths from the bar area and wet them," Garrett shouted. "Use them to breathe through."

His eyes teared up from the smoke. "Where is it?" He ran his fingers along the brick wall. Finally, at the Big Dipper, he felt a notch at one star. He pressed the button. The brick gave way. He pushed the concealed doorway open.

"It was good of Fiona to have our meeting at midnight. Darkness will help hide us."

Garrett paused at a weapon safe in the corner. He grabbed a hunting knife and a rifle. "Laurel, here you go." He shoved an old Colt .45 at her. "You couldn't have had an Uzi in here, could you, old man?" He pulled a Bowie knife from a drawer and pressed it into James's hands. Even with his injuries, he gripped the weapon.

"Get them out," James choked. "Leave me." He passed out.

"Not on your life." Garrett heaved James over his shoulder in a fireman's carry. "Laurel, let's go."

She clutched Molly to her and followed him out through a short passageway leading up to a tunnel. The gradient rose.

A dim lighting system lit the narrow path. Garrett struggled with James's weight. At the end of the tunnel there was a small door. A key dangled at the edge.

"Thanks, James." Garrett grabbed the key and unlocked the door. It led into what looked like a storage shed. Garrett recognized it from his previous visits.

"I never knew this passageway was here," Laurel whispered.

Garrett didn't turn the light on. He laid James on the ground and propped him up against the rough wooden wall. Garrett peered through a small window in the shed.

Laurel stood at his side, her entire body stiff with resolve.

Flames erupted from James's house, searing through brick and wood. Loud crackling overwhelmed the quiet neighborhood. Smoke billowed into the air and the fire painted the midnight sky red.

Another explosion rocketed through the house.

"That one waited for us to get out," Garrett whispered to her. "Not bad, Léon."

"He's on our side. He can help."

"Rafe Vargas is out there, too." At Laurel's questioning glance, Garrett added, "Another CTC operative. We aren't alone."

"If they haven't been caught," Laurel said. "What's the plan?"

"I'm going out there. Fiona's not getting away with this."

He gripped the old Remington hunting rifle he'd snagged from the safe. "Stay here," he ordered Laurel. "Protect them."

She gripped Garrett's arm. "Be careful. Come back to me."

He gave her a small smile. "Count on it." Then his gaze turned serious. "Have you got your weapon?"

She pulled out the Colt. "I know what to do with it."

He kissed her quickly. "I love you. I should have told you before." Garrett raced out of the building.

A lone figure, carrying an M16, emerged from the smoke. Fiona pointed the weapon at Garrett. "I don't leave witnesses."

Garrett didn't hesitate. He raised his weapon. Before he could get off a shot, a bevy of bullets tore across his body.

He blinked and looked down, then sank to his knees.

Chapter Twelve

A spray of bullets sounded from outside, and then another volley came a moment later. Some pierced the shed. Laurel dragged her father to the ground and covered Molly with her body.

The little girl cried out in fear.

Laurel's heart raced. Garrett hadn't had an automatic weapon.

Please, God, let him live. "Molly," Laurel ordered. "Get over by Grandpa. Hide in the darkest corner."

Molly crawled over toward James, and Laurel quickly stacked a wheelbarrow and other tools in front of them. "Stay here. Take care of each other."

She slipped some metal spikes and a small scythe next to her barely conscious father. It was all she could do for weapons.

"Back up Garrett if he's still—" Her father paused and looked at Molly. "You can't let Fiona escape. Do what needs to be done."

Laurel grabbed the old .45. Handguns were hard to shoot accurately. She'd need to get close.

She opened the shed door slowly, only to see Fiona standing over Garrett's prone body. Behind them, the bodies of her two minions lay on the grass near the burning house.

Fiona pointed her weapon at Garrett again. "You've been damn tough to kill, Bradley, but this head shot ought to do it."

Laurel didn't hesitate. She aimed and fired. Once. Twice. And again, until the gun was empty. Fiona jerked, but she didn't go down. "Stupid woman," Fiona taunted. "Never heard of Kevlar? You're going to pay for that."

Laurel dropped her weapon. She had one chance. If she could get the right angle—

"Aunt Laurel, Aunt Laurel. Come quick. Grandpa's not moving." Molly ran into the yard.

Fiona met Laurel's horror-struck gaze. The woman smiled and swept her gun around, pointing it at the little girl. "Guess the rug rat's next."

Just as Fiona was about to squeeze the trigger, a shot rang out from behind her. The bullet struck her in the head. She hit the ground hard, the wound fatal.

Molly screamed and cowered on the ground.

Laurel's eyes widened. Garrett's arm shook and he dropped the Remington. "She's not the only one who's heard of Kevlar." He coughed. With that, his head dropped to the grass. Laurel grabbed Molly and raced over to Garrett.

Blood pooled at two gunshot wounds.

He glanced down at the red seeping through his shirt. "I needed a bigger size." He looked up at Laurel. "I'm sorry."

Sirens grew louder in the distance.

"Garrett, you're going to be fine. Just hang on. Help is on the way," she said softly, then gasped as his eyes fluttered closed. "Garrett, no!"

"Sheriff Garrett?" Molly whispered. "Please don't go away."

"I'll try, sugar." He coughed.

Laurel leaned down closer. "You told me you loved me, Garrett. You can't leave me now. I love you, too."

There was no response. His chest barely rose.

"Oh, God, no." She didn't know what to do. The vest might be stanching the blood. She needed help.

Suddenly, a crush of police cars, fire engines and ambulances skidded to the curbs. Various personnel carrying hoses, guns and medical equipment came around the house. Laurel yelled to them, "We need help here. A man's been shot!"

She clutched Molly tightly as tears streamed down their faces.

Two paramedics rushed over. "Move back."

Laurel jerked away, hiding Molly's face against her own chest. "My father is in the shed over there." Laurel pointed out the small bullet-ridden structure. "He's badly hurt. Please help him, too."

The paramedics called another of the backup teams to check out the shed.

The yard was complete chaos. The firemen futilely fought the blaze, but whatever had been used to blow up the house did not back off easily.

"Another injured," a cop shouted. "Guy's pinned under a wall."

Men raced around the house. The police hovered over the paramedics, watching them work on Garrett. Others checked the gathering crowds. Still more hurried to where Fiona and the other two bodies lay.

"Hey, this one's alive," someone called out, bending

over one of the men lying near Fiona's body. "I need a medic, quick."

Laurel couldn't tell if it was Léon. She hoped so.

"Please, Garrett. Please make it," she said, clutching Molly to her.

More responders dragged gurneys across the grass to the injured. Laurel stood back, holding Molly, her attention split between Garrett and the activity in the shed. She prayed her father wouldn't come out in a black bag.

What seemed an eternity later, Garrett, her father and Léon were all loaded into different ambulances.

Laurel carried Molly over to the back of the one carrying Garrett and tried to get inside.

"You can't, ma'am."

"Why not? That's my father and Garrett is my...my... fiancé."

A police detective walked up beside her. "Lady, as the only person still standing on a field with multiple dead bodies, you have a lot of explaining to do. I can see the gunshot residue on your hand. We're not letting you near anybody. The kid will have to go with Child Protective Services."

Laurel panicked and held Molly close. "No, she may not be safe without special protection. Please, she's been through so much. Let me call a family she trusts to come take care of her."

"Aunt Laurel," Molly cried. "I want to stay with you. Don't make me leave."

Laurel knelt down in front of Molly so they were face-to-face. "Molly, honey, I have to go with these policemen for a little while to tell them what happened. It's not a place for children."

She shook her head. "You said you wouldn't leave me. Not like Mommy and Daddy."

Laurel couldn't control the tears. "I'm going to call Daniel and Raven. You can stay with them. You could play with the twins, too, and their doggy."

Molly bit her lip. "I like Raven a lot. She gives me cookies. Daniel's nice, too." Then she shook her head. "But I want you and Sheriff Garrett."

Gripping Molly's hands in hers, Laurel met the little girl's gaze. "Please, Molly Magoo. Can you be brave for me one more time?"

"Like Sheriff Garrett?"

Laurel squeezed her niece's hands. "Like Sheriff Garrett. Go to Daniel and Raven."

"You'll come back for me. Promise?"

Somehow she would. "I promise." Laurel looked up at the officer. "Please, let her go to them. You'll understand what's going on soon enough. I cannot have her put through any more trauma."

The detective's brow furrowed. "I got kids of my own," he relented. "Give me the family's info and I'll check them out. Otherwise, the girl goes with CPS."

The police station reeked of the sights and smells of nighttime indigents and criminals. Molly wouldn't let go of Laurel's hand.

She desperately wanted to pace the walkways of the police station, but she had to shield Molly. She glanced over at a tired-looking woman standing in the corner, ever watchful. If Daniel didn't arrive soon, CPS might just take Molly away. Laurel's heart broke at the idea of being separated from her niece.

How could she explain everything that had happened? Would the cops even believe her?

Finally, the door opened and Daniel strode inside, along with another man wearing a patch over one eye, who looked as if he'd been on the wrong end of a fight. She recognized him from somewhere. He walked over and had a few words with the officer assigned to watch Laurel. Her interrogation would start as soon as Molly left.

Laurel finally placed the man's face and scowled. "Exactly *who* is your friend?"

Daniel looked back at the man who was now approaching them. "Laurel, this is Rafe. He's part of CTC, the organization I work for. He was stationed outside the house, but got buried by a wall."

"Is there a problem?" Rafe asked seriously.

"I don't know," she said, her voice full of suspicion. "I saw you driving the ambulance with that man, Léon, inside. You didn't go the same direction as the other ambulances. Why?"

Rafe lowered his voice when he spoke. "Léon is one of ours, too. I took him to some medical facilities that were a little more…discreet. His recovery will take a while and we wanted him safe."

"Great," she snapped. "What about Garrett and my father? What about keeping them safe?" She knew she sounded like an ungrateful witch, but no one would even tell her if Garrett and her father were alive or dead.

"Garrett and your father are alive," Rafe said, "but in critical condition. We have guards both inside and outside their doors, as well as throughout the hospital, keeping watch for intruders. My boss is trying to keep the feds and agency people out of this so they don't have access to Garrett. If they identify him as a fugitive before we prove his innocence, the government will claim him."

Laurel rubbed her face with her hands. "They're alive." Her knees shook.

"I've brought enough evidence that you should be out of here soon, Laurel. Just be patient. I'll take Molly now, and Rafe will wait and handle bail or whatever comes up. He won't let you down, Laurel. I swear it."

Tears filled Laurel's eyes as she hugged Molly and sent her off with Daniel. "Please keep her safe."

"Daniel would give his life for Molly. He'll guard her well."

Just then, a policeman walked over. "Ms. McCallister, it's time."

FROM SOMEWHERE FAR OFF, Garrett heard a sweet female voice calling to him.

"Garrett, please wake up."

He felt a gentle touch on his forehead, but couldn't make much sense out of the soothing, soft words being whispered in his ear.

The dreams had been haunting him again. Strange dreams, where Lisa and Ella were running to him, holding him close, but suddenly they were waving goodbye. *No! Don't go.* Something was wrong. It was very wrong. He fought his way toward consciousness.

The dream changed, colors swirling and spinning in his mind, and this time he was reaching out for Laurel and Molly. He tried to reach them, but they were so far away. They were leaving, too. Sadness in their eyes. The gray returned and pulled him back into the darkness.

The whispering continued, more urgently this time.

The voices were louder. Why wouldn't they leave him alone?

"Garrett. Wake up."

He strained to understand, but each time he tried to open his eyes, they didn't respond at all.

"Come back to me now. You can do this."

Laurel? Was that Laurel trying to get him to do something? He struggled again, forcing the fogginess in his mind away.

A firm hand gripped his, as if to will him to do something. His eyelids were so heavy, but somehow he forced them open for the briefest second. The blaze of sunlight burned his eyes and he groaned, flinching from the light. Even that slight movement sent a spear of fiery pain through his chest.

"He moved!" Laurel yelled. "His eyes opened for a second. Get the doctor in here fast." A firm hand gripped his. "Come on, Garrett. Open your eyes."

"Hurts," he rasped.

"Shut the blinds and turn off the lights. It's too bright," Laurel ordered, then suddenly laughed. "Oh, my God, Garrett. You're waking up. I thought I'd lost you. I love you so very much."

Laurel's voice pulled him from the darkness. He needed to reach her. He had to reach her. He fought with everything inside to open his eyes.

A halo around beautiful brown hair slowly came into focus. He blinked again. She was beautiful. Like an angel.

"Laurel?" His voice sounded strange, hoarse, and when he tried to raise his hand, that blasted pain speared through his chest again.

"Don't move and don't try to talk, Garrett. They just

took the breathing tube out." She put the tiniest ice chip on his tongue to soothe his throat. "You've been in a coma. But you're going to be okay."

Visions came back to him. A little girl holding Laurel's hand, so small and scared. Then outside, in the darkness, an AK-47 pointed at her. "Molly?"

"She's safe. You saved her."

"Fiona?"

Laurel's face went cold. "Dead."

"Good." His eyes closed. "You're all safe." Everything went black and this time he didn't fight it.

LAUREL SAGGED IN the chair when Garrett lost consciousness again.

The doctor strode in.

"The nurse said the patient moved." The man's voice was skeptical. "He looks pretty out of it now. What happened?"

Laurel stood. "He woke up. He spoke to me. He knew me. He remembered some of what happened the night he was shot."

"I didn't expect that much, so it's a good sign. He's been unconscious for two weeks, so don't expect him to go dancing anytime soon." The neurologist leaned over Garrett and checked his vital signs, then his bandages. "The bullet wounds to his chest are healing nicely. His latest MRI showed the swelling has gone down."

"I knew he'd come back to me."

The doctor smiled at her. "Family often knows best. The more you stayed and talked to him, the more you kept his brain stimulated. He may not have known what you were saying, but even in a coma, there is some level of communication happening, especially among loved ones. Your dedication has been important to his recovery. You're going to make him a great wife."

Laurel gulped. She'd never cleared up the misconception that Garrett was her fiancé. The hospital staff never would have let her stay as often or as long as she had.

Legally, she and Garrett weren't family, but in every way that mattered, Garrett had become an integral part of her life. So much had happened. She prayed he'd still want her when he awoke and he could make different choices than the ones she hoped he would.

A short time after the doctor left, Laurel gripped Garrett's hand. If what the doctor said was true, had Garrett heard all the times she'd told him she loved him? There hadn't been time before. But she could no longer imagine life without this man.

"Laurel?" His eyes fluttered open again. With the lights off and window shades drawn, he was able to keep his eyelids somewhat open. "I thought I dreamed—"

His voice gave out and Laurel quickly gave him another ice chip. Several more, spread over the next five minutes, finally allowed him to speak without too bad a rasp to his voice.

"Did James make it?" he asked, watching her warily.

She smiled. "Yes, but he's hurt badly. The burns were…" Laurel stopped, unable to speak further.

"Is he still in the hospital?"

"No. Not this one, anyway. The authorities took him away for a debriefing. I don't know when I'll see him. Your friends at CTC are working on it."

"I'm sorry. You haven't heard anything?"

"Nothing specific, other than that they're angry that he lied about you under oath. It will take time for him to win back anyone's trust. At least my sister's evidence cleared you both of the treason charges. The story has been all over the papers. You're a hero."

"Yeah, right. I almost got you all killed."

"No, Garrett," Laurel insisted, "Fiona almost got us all killed. I've been afraid to take any chances ever since my mother died. My father drilled into Ivy and me that we were only to rely on ourselves. Not anyone else, and sure as hell not him." Laurel hesitated. "Yet a few weeks ago I found myself relying on a man I didn't even know, and every time you proved yourself worthy of trusting."

"You mean when I wasn't lying to you or sneaking out without telling you."

"Yeah, well, we can work on that."

"It was always for your own good," Garrett said.

"Like I said, we'll work on it. Don't push your luck, Sheriff. I was giving you the benefit of the doubt, and you're blowing it big-time."

"Come here." He pulled her gently toward him.

Laurel closed her eyes and leaned forward on the bed. Afraid to jar the wound on his chest, she rested her head gently on Garrett's arm. She longed for those arms to surround her again; she longed for him to hold her close and just talk, just to hear his voice tell her again that he loved her. She wanted to hear him sing that silly ant song once more to Molly in his deep voice. The one that made her feel safe down to her soul.

He stroked her head with his hand. "Why didn't you leave? You didn't have to stay watching over me."

Had he changed his mind about her? She couldn't stop the tears from falling down her cheeks. "I didn't have anywhere else to be," she said. "I figured hanging out in a hospital with you would be a good way to spend Christmas. It's already decorated for the holidays and

Molly's having a wonderful time at Daniel and Raven's. The I-want-a-puppy hints are coming fast and furious. I think a dog is even beating out the princess palace she asked for all year."

Garrett blinked. "Wait a minute. Back up. It's Christmas?"

"Not quite, but close. It's next week."

His eyes went wide. "How long have I been out?"

"Thirteen days, seven hours and twenty-three minutes, but who's counting?" she said, trying for a nonchalance she did not feel.

"You should have left me here," he said. "Molly's so afraid Santa won't be able to find her this year. She needs some normalcy back in her life. She needs you."

His words pierced her heart. Laurel pulled back. "You don't want me here?"

Garrett swallowed and looked at her. "I...I want what's best for you. And Molly."

"You are what's best for me. Can't you see that?"

"I didn't protect you," he said. "You could have died because I didn't plan well enough ahead."

She laughed incredulously. "Garrett, I'm the one who contacted Fiona. If I'd trusted you—"

He gripped her hands. "If we'd trusted each other."

Laurel rose from the bed slowly. "Is this really where we are? Fighting over something this stupid?" She stepped closer. "I am going to give you an ultimatum. Answer it wrong and I will walk away forever."

He struggled to sit up in the bed. "Wait. What are you talking about?"

"I'm talking about us. I love you. Do you hear me? No doubts, no questions on my side. You once told me the same thing, but you thought you were going off to die."

"Laurel—"

"I am not done, mister. Not by a long shot. Derek Bradley's name has been cleared, so if that's the life you want, you can go back to the clandestine, lonely life you led before. But you have a choice. The mayor of Trouble says that you can continue as the sheriff."

Garrett sat staring at her. "The mayor? The mayor hates me because I'm onto his tricks."

"Oh, Daniel had a little talk with that mayor, and he resigned. Hondo took over the job, and he said you can be sheriff as long as he's in office."

Garrett chuckled, then turned serious. "Is that the end of the options available to me? Because it's not a hard choice." Laurel could barely breathe. "Do you think I'd choose anyone or anything but you, Laurel? Where's your faith?"

She couldn't stop the smile from spreading across her face.

"Say the words. When guns aren't blazing and you're not running off to certain death. I need to hear it."

Garrett met her gaze, unwavering, serious. "I love you, Laurel McCallister. I will always love you."

She quivered against him and laid her head on his chest. "I won't ever let you go."

Epilogue

Garrett sat on the floor and placed the last fake flower in the garden of Molly's princess palace.

Laurel walked up to him and handed him a cup of coffee. "You shouldn't be drinking this."

"I won't tell the doctors if you don't." He took a sip of the dark brew and nearly groaned in pleasure. "Some assembly required? That's what the box said. How long have I been at it?"

"Six hours." Laurel chuckled.

"I just hope she likes it. Molly needs some joy."

Laurel knelt down beside him. "She feels safe with you, Garrett. And loved. That's all she needs."

The chime of the clock sounded through the house.

"It's six o'clock."

Garrett struggled to get up off of the floor. Laurel held out her hand to steady him. "Take it easy," she said, putting her hands on his waist. "I just got you back."

He kissed her lips, drinking in the taste of her. He stroked his hand down her cheek. "Have I told you lately that you've made my life wonderful?" Her cheeks flushed. "I'm serious. You didn't just love me—you brought Christmas back. You brought joy into this ranch house."

"I could say the same about you, Garrett Galloway."

Laurel wrapped her arms around him, taking his lips. Garrett let himself get lost in her touch. If it weren't for the fact that this was Christmas Day, he'd drag her back to their bedroom and stay there all day long.

A soft knock forced him to raise his head. "Who is that?"

Garrett walked to the door, pulling his Beretta from atop the refrigerator. Slowly he opened the door.

A thin man in a red suit stood on the steps.

"Santa?"

Molly's sleepy voice came from just outside the living room.

The man walked inside.

"Dad?" Laurel whispered.

"Grandpa!" Molly raced to her grandfather.

He swung her up in the air with a grimace. "Molly Magoo!"

She wrapped her arms around him and hugged him tight. "Grandpa, I thought you were gone to heaven like Mommy and Daddy. And Matthew and Michaela."

James hugged Molly and met Laurel's and Garrett's gazes. His eyes were wet. Molly touched one of his tears. "It's okay, Grandpa. They're watching over us all the time. Aunt Laurel and Sheriff Garrett said so."

"I know." The old man cleared his throat. "Hope there's room for an old man on Christmas morning."

"It's Christmas!" Molly wiggled until James put her down. She looked around the room, past the princess palace. Her head dropped. "My letter didn't reach him."

Laurel knelt beside Molly. "Look at the beautiful princess palace. Santa knew exactly what you wanted."

"It's beautiful," she said, tears streaming down her face. "But I wanted to change my Christmas wish list."

Molly's tears broke Garrett's heart. "What do you want, sugar?" he asked gently.

"I want a family," she said, her voice small. "I know my mommy and daddy can't come back, but I don't want to be alone."

Garrett picked Molly up into his arms. He kissed her temple. "I think I can do something about that wish." He walked over to Laurel. "Wait right here."

He walked out the door and within minutes returned with a wrapped gift the size of a bread box. "Sit on the sofa, Molly. You, too, Laurel."

Garrett's nerves were stretched thin. James stood in the corner, a satisfied grin on his face. The old spy knew too much.

With his hand bracing himself, Garrett eased himself down on one knee. "Open the box, Molly."

She lifted the lid and peeked inside. A smile lit her face. A russet-and-white puppy poked its head out.

"For me?"

"You need a friend on this ranch, don't you think?"

Molly hugged the puppy to her. The mixed breed licked her face. "What's his name?"

"Whatever you want it to be, Molly."

She stroked his soft fur. "I love him, Sheriff Garrett."

"What do you think, Laurel?"

Her eyes were wet with tears. "I love him as much as I love you."

"Then maybe you should check out what's around his neck?"

Laurel grabbed the squirming bundle of fur and looked

at his collar. A ring swung back and forth. She stilled. "Garrett?"

"I love you, Laurel. I love Molly. Will you marry me?"

"Yes!" Molly shouted, hugging Garrett around the neck. "We want to marry you. Right, Aunt Laurel?"

"Right." Laurel's voice was thick with emotion. "I do."

"So we're going to live here forever and forever. You, me and Aunt Laurel. And Pumpkin Pie?"

"Who?"

"My doggy. His name is Pumpkin Pie. He told me."

"Yes, sugar, we'll all live together. Sometimes here, but sometimes in town. In Trouble, Texas."

Molly grinned up at them. "I think my daddy and mommy in heaven would like that. They told me almost every day that I was an angel always looking for trouble." She flung herself into Garrett's arms. "And we found it."

Garrett met Laurel's gaze over Molly's head. "Okay with you? If we're a family?"

She slipped the ring on her left hand and kissed his lips gently. "A family for Christmas is the best present ever."

* * * * *

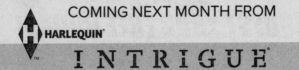

COMING NEXT MONTH FROM

HARLEQUIN

INTRIGUE

Available December 16, 2014

#1539 MIDNIGHT RIDER
Big "D" Dads: The Daltons • by Joanna Wayne
When her search for a killer leads to danger and bull rider Cannon Dalton, homicide detective Brittany Garner will face her toughest case yet...catch her long-lost twin's killer, and try *not* to fall for the man who might be her infant niece's father...

#1540 MOUNTAIN RETREAT • by Cassie Miles
After being held captive, CIA agent Nick Corelli is finally reunited with his fiancée, Sidney Parker. Explaining his six-month absence is the least of Nick's problems when someone from the agency is determined to make them both disappear...permanently.

#1541 THE SHERIFF
West Texas Watchmen • by Angi Morgan
Mysterious lights, a missing woman, a lifelong secret revealed...all under a star-studded West Texas sky. Sheriff Pete Morrison must protect a gorgeous witness, Andrea Allen, from gun smugglers and...herself.

#1542 GUT INSTINCT
The Campbells of Creek Bend • by Barb Han
Sparks fly when FBI agent Luke Campbell and his ex-wife, Julie Davis, work one-on-one to hunt a serial killer. Can Luke regain her trust and save her from a skillful murderer before it's too late?

#1543 THE MARSHAL • by Adrienne Giordano
To find his mother's killer, Deputy United States Marshal Brent Thompson partners with sexy private investigator Jenna Hayward. Will their combined need to capture a killer risk both their lives?

#1544 INFILTRATION
Omega Sector • by Janie Crouch
Agent Cameron Branson is forced to bring Sophia Reardon, the woman he once loved, into his dark, undercover world. And the chances of them getting out alive have never looked more slim...

REQUEST YOUR FREE BOOKS!
2 FREE NOVELS PLUS 2 FREE GIFTS!

H HARLEQUIN®

INTRIGUE®

BREATHTAKING ROMANTIC SUSPENSE

YES! Please send me 2 FREE Harlequin Intrigue® novels and my 2 FREE gifts (gifts are worth about $10). After receiving them, if I don't wish to receive any more books, I can return the shipping statement marked "cancel." If I don't cancel, I will receive 6 brand-new novels every month and be billed just $4.74 per book in the U.S. or $5.24 per book in Canada. That's a savings of at least 14% off the cover price! It's quite a bargain! Shipping and handling is just 50¢ per book in the U.S. and 75¢ per book in Canada.* I understand that accepting the 2 free books and gifts places me under no obligation to buy anything. I can always return a shipment and cancel at any time. Even if I never buy another book, the two free books and gifts are mine to keep forever.

182/382 HDN F42N

Name	(PLEASE PRINT)	

Address		Apt. #

City	State/Prov.	Zip/Postal Code

Signature (if under 18, a parent or guardian must sign)

Mail to the **Harlequin® Reader Service:**
IN U.S.A.: P.O. Box 1867, Buffalo, NY 14240-1867
IN CANADA: P.O. Box 609, Fort Erie, Ontario L2A 5X3
**Are you a subscriber to Harlequin Intrigue books
and want to receive the larger-print edition?
Call 1-800-873-8635 or visit www.ReaderService.com.**

* Terms and prices subject to change without notice. Prices do not include applicable taxes. Sales tax applicable in N.Y. Canadian residents will be charged applicable taxes. Offer not valid in Quebec. This offer is limited to one order per household. Not valid for current subscribers to Harlequin Intrigue books. All orders subject to credit approval. Credit or debit balances in a customer's account(s) may be offset by any other outstanding balance owed by or to the customer. Please allow 4 to 6 weeks for delivery. Offer available while quantities last.

Your Privacy—The Harlequin® Reader Service is committed to protecting your privacy. Our Privacy Policy is available online at www.ReaderService.com or upon request from the Harlequin Reader Service.

We make a portion of our mailing list available to reputable third parties that offer products we believe may interest you. If you prefer that we not exchange your name with third parties, or if you wish to clarify or modify your communication preferences, please visit us at www.ReaderService.com/consumerschoice or write to us at Harlequin Reader Service Preference Service, P.O. Box 9062, Buffalo, NY 14269. Include your complete name and address.

HI13R

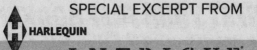
"The woman in Greenleaf Bar was you?"

"You don't remember?"

"Vaguely."

He struggled to put things in perspective. That had been a hell of a night. He'd stopped at the first bar he'd come to after leaving the rodeo. A blonde had sat down next to him. As best he remembered, he'd given her an earful about the rodeo, life and death as he'd become more and more inebriated.

She must have offered him a ride back to his hotel since his truck had still been at the bar when he'd gone looking for it the next morning. If Brit was telling the truth, the woman must have gone into the motel with him and they'd ended up doing the deed.

If so, he'd been a total jerk. She'd been as drunk as him and driven or she'd willingly taken a huge risk.

Hard to imagine the woman staring at him now ever

being that careless or impulsive.

"Is that your normal pattern, Mr. Dalton?" Brit asked. "Use a woman to satisfy your physical needs and then ride off to the next rodeo?"

"That's a little like the armadillo calling the squirrel roadkill, isn't it? I'm sure I didn't coerce you into my bed if I was so drunk I can't remember the experience."

"I can assure you that you're nowhere near that irresistible. I have never been in your bed."

"Whew. That's a relief. I'd have probably died of frostbite."

"This isn't a joking matter."

"I'm well aware. But I'm not the enemy here, so you can quit talking to me like I just climbed out from under a slimy rock. If you're not Kimmie's mother, who is?"

"My twin sister, Sylvie Hamm."

Twin sisters. That explained Brit's attitude. Probably considered her sister a victim of the drunken sex urges he didn't remember. It also explained why Brit Garner looked familiar.

"So why is it I'm not having this conversation with Sylvie?"

"She's dead."

Find out what happens next in
MIDNIGHT RIDER
by Joanna Wayne,
available January 2015 wherever
Harlequin Intrigue® books and ebooks are sold.